THE DEMON DETHRONED...

John Gabriel came up to me. His voice when he spoke was thick, the words were slurred.

He laughed, a drunken sort of laugh.

"I told you Isabella Charteris was just like any other girl. Her head may be in the stars, but her feet are set in clay all right."

"What are you talking about?" I said sharply. "Have you been drinking?"

He let out another laugh.

"That's a good one! No, I haven't been drinking. I told you she wasn't a saint—not with a mouth like that....She's human all right...."

"Look here, Gabriel," I said furiously, "what have you been up to?"

He let out a cackle of laughter.

"I've been enjoying myself, old boy," he said. "In my own way—and a damned good way too."

"Christie can build ingenius puzzles ... and plot keeps this one going."

—*The New York Times*

Books by Agatha Christie
writing as Mary Westmacott
from Jove

MARY WESTMACOTT
known to millions as
AGATHA CHRISTIE

THE ROSE
AND THE
YEW TREE

JOVE BOOKS, NEW YORK

The moment of the rose and the moment of the yew tree
are of equal duration—T. S. ELIOT

This Jove book contains the complete
text of the original edition.

THE ROSE AND THE YEW TREE

A Jove Book / published by arrangement with
Rosalind Hicks

PRINTING HISTORY
Two previous Dell editions
New Dell edition / July 1982
Jove edition / January 1988

ISBN: 0-515-09381-5

Jove Books are published by The Berkley Publishing Group,
200 Madison Avenue, New York, New York 10016.
The name "JOVE" and the "J" logo
are trademarks belonging to Jove Publications, Inc.

PRINTED IN THE UNITED STATES OF AMERICA

10   9   8   7   6   5   4   3

PRELUDE

I was in Paris when Parfitt, my man, came to me and said that a lady had called to see me. She said, he added, that it was very important.

I had formed by then the habit of never seeing people without an appointment. People who call to see you about urgent business are nearly invariably people who wish for financial assistance. The people who are in real need of financial assistance, on the other hand, hardly ever come and ask for it.

I asked Parfitt what my visitor's name was, and he proffered a card. The card said: Catherine Yougoubian—a name I had never heard of and which, frankly, I did not much fancy. I revised my idea that she needed financial assistance and deduced instead that she had something to sell—probably one of those spurious antiques which command a better price when they are brought by hand and forced on the unwilling buyer with the aid of voluble patter.

I said I was sorry that I could not see Madame Yougoubian, but she could write and state her business.

Parfitt inclined his head and withdrew. He is very reliable—an invalid such as I am needs a reliable attendant—and I had not the slightest doubt that the matter was now disposed of. Much to my astonishment, however, Parfitt reappeared. The lady, he said, was very insistent. It was a matter of life and death and concerned an old friend of mine.

Whereupon my curiosity was suddenly aroused. Not by the message—that was a fairly obvious gambit; life and death and the old friend are the usual counters in the game. No, what stimulated my curiosity was the behavior of Parfitt. It was not like Parfitt to come back with a message of that kind.

I jumped, quite wrongly, to the conclusion that Catherine Yougoubian was incredibly beautiful, or at any rate unusually attractive. Nothing else, I thought, would explain Parfitt's behavior.

And since a man is always a man, even if he be fifty and a cripple, I fell into the snare. I wanted to see this radiant creature who could overcome the defences of the impeccable Parfitt.

So I told him to bring the lady up—and when Catherine Yougoubian entered the room, revulsion of feeling nearly took my breath away!

True, I understand Parfitt's behavior well enough now. His judgment of human nature is quite unerring. He recognized in Catherine that persistence of temperament against which, in the end, all defences fall. Wisely, he capitulated straight away and saved himself a long and wearying battle. For Catherine Yougoubian has the persistence of a sledge hammer and the monotony of an oxyacetylene blowpipe: combined with the wearing effect of water dropping on a stone! Time is infinite for her if she wishes to achieve her object. She would have sat determinedly in my entrance hall all day. She is one of those women who have room in their heads for one idea only—which gives them an enormous advantage over less single-minded individuals.

As I say, the shock I got when she entered the room was tremendous. I was all keyed up to behold beauty. Instead, the woman who entered was monumentally, almost awe-inspiringly, plain. Not ugly, mark you; ugliness has its own rhythm, its own mode of attack, but Catherine had a large flat face like a pancake—a kind of desert of a face. Her mouth was wide and had a slight—a very slight—moustache on its upper lip. Her eyes were small and dark and made one think of inferior currants in an inferior bun. Her hair was abundant, ill-confined, and pre-eminently greasy. Her figure was so nondescript that it was practically not a figure at all. Her clothes covered her adequately and fitted her nowhere. She appeared neither destitute nor opulent. She had a determined jaw and, as I heard when she opened her mouth, a harsh and unlovely voice.

I threw a glance of deep reproach at Parfitt who met it

imperturbably. He was clearly of the opinion that, as usual, he knew best.

"Madame Yougoubian, sir," he said, and retired, shutting the door and leaving me at the mercy of this determined-looking female.

Catherine advanced upon me purposefully. I had never felt so helpless, so conscious of my crippled state. This was a woman from whom it would be advisable to run away, and I could not run.

She spoke in a loud firm voice.

"Please—if you will be so good—you must come with me, please?"

It was less of a request than a command.

"I beg your pardon?" I said, startled.

"I do not speak the English too good, I am afraid. But there is not time to lose—no, no time at all. It is to Mr. Gabriel I ask you to come. He is very ill. Soon, very soon, he dies, and he has asked for you. So to see him you must come at once."

I stared at her. Frankly, I thought she was crazy. The name Gabriel made no impression upon me at all, partly, I daresay, because of her pronunciation. It did not sound in the least like Gabriel. But even if it had sounded like it, I do not think that it would have stirred a chord. It was all so long ago. It must have been ten years since I had even thought of John Gabriel.

"You say someone is dying? Someone—er—that I know?"

She cast at me a look of infinite reproach.

"But yes, you know him—you know him well—and he asks for you."

She was so positive that I began to rack my brains. What name had she said? Gable? Galbraith? I had known a Galbraith, a mining engineer. Only casually, it is true; it seemed in the highest degree unlikely that he should ask to see me on his deathbed. Yet it is a tribute to Catherine's force of character that I did not doubt for a moment the truth of her statement.

"What name did you say?" I asked. "Galbraith?"

"No—no. Gabriel. *Gabriel!*"

I stared. This time I got the word right, but it only conjured up a mental vision of the Angel Gabriel with a large pair of wings. The vision fitted in well enough with Catherine Yougoubian. She had a resemblance to the type of earnest woman usually to be found kneeling in the extreme lefthand corner of an early Italian Primitive. She had that peculiar simplicity of feature combined with the look of ardent devotion.

She added, persistently, doggedly, *"John* Gabriel—" and I got it!

It all came back to me. I felt giddy and slightly sick. St. Loo, and the old ladies, and Milly Burt, and John Gabriel with his ugly dynamic little face, rocking gently back on his heels. And Rupert, tall and handsome like a young god. And, of course, Isabella. . . .

I remembered the last time I had seen John Gabriel in Zagrade and what had happened there, and I felt rising in me a surging red tide of anger and loathing. . . .

"So he's dying, is he?" I asked savagely. "I'm delighted to hear it!"

"Pardon?"

There are things that you cannot very well repeat when someone says "Pardon?" politely to you. Catherine Yougoubian looked utterly uncomprehending. I merely said:

"You say he is dying?"

"Yes. He is in pain—in terrible pain."

Well, I was delighted to hear that, too. No pain that John Gabriel could suffer would atone for what he had done. But I felt unable to say so to one who was evidently John Gabriel's devoted worshipper.

What was there about the fellow, I wondered irritably, that always made women fall for him? He was ugly as sin. He was pretentious, vulgar, boastful. He had brains of a kind, and he was, in certain circumstances (low circumstances!) good company. He had humor. But none of these are really characteristics that appeal to women very much.

Catherine broke in upon my thoughts.

"You will come, please? You will come quickly? There is no time to lose."

I pulled myself together.

"I'm sorry, my dear lady," I said, "but I'm afraid I cannot accompany you."

"But he asks for you," she persisted.

"I'm not coming," I said.

"You do not understand," said Catherine. "He is ill. He is dying; and he asks for you."

I braced myself for the fight. I had already begun to realize (what Parfitt had realized at the first glance) that Catherine Yougoubian did not give up easily.

"You are making a mistake," I said. "John Gabriel is not a friend of mine."

She nodded her head vigorously.

"But yes—but yes. He read your name in the paper—it say you are here as member of the Commission—and he say I am to find out where you live and to get you to come. And please you must come quick—very quick—for the doctor say very soon now. So will you come at once, please?"

It seemed to me that I had got to be frank. I said:

"He may rot in Hell for all I care!"

"Pardon?"

She looked at me anxiously, wrinkling her long nose, amiable, trying to understand. . . .

"John Gabriel," I said slowly and clearly, "is *not* a friend of mine. He is a man I hate—*hate!* Now do you understand?"

She blinked. It seemed to me that at last she was beginning to get there.

"You say—", she said it slowly, like a child repeating a difficult lesson, "you say that—you—hate—John Gabriel? Is that what you say, please?"

"That's right," I said.

She smiled—a maddening smile.

"No, no," she said indulgently, "that is not possible. . . . No one could hate John Gabriel. He is very great—very good—man. All of us who know him, we die for him gladly."

"Good God," I cried, exasperated. "What's the man ever done that people should feel like that about him?"

Well, I had asked for it! She forgot the urgency of her mission. She sat down, she pushed back a loop of greasy hair from her forehead, her eyes shone with enthusiasm, she opened her mouth, and words poured from her. . . . .

She spoke, I think, for about a quarter of an hour. Sometimes she was incomprehensible, stumbling with the difficulties of the spoken word. Sometimes her words flowed in a clear stream. But the whole performance had the effect of a great epic.

She spoke with reverence, with awe, with humility, with worship. She spoke of John Gabriel as one speaks of a Messiah—and that clearly was what he was to her. She said things of him that to me seemed wildly fantastic and wholly impossible. She spoke of a man tender, brave, and strong. A leader and a succorer. She spoke of one who risked death that others might live; of one who hated cruelty and injustice with a white and burning flame. He was to her a Prophet, a King, a Saviour—one who could give to people courage that they did not know they had, and strength that they did not know they possessed. He had been tortured more than once; crippled, half-killed; but somehow his maimed body had overcome its disabilities by sheer willpower, and he had continued to perform the impossible.

"You do not know, you say, what he has done?" she ended. "But everyone knows Father Clement—*everyone*!"

I stared—for what she said was true. Everyone has heard of Father Clement. His is a name to conjure with, even if some people hold that it is only a name—a myth—and that the real man has never existed.

How shall I describe the legend of Father Clement? Imagine a mixture of Richard Coeur de Lion and Father Damien and Lawrence of Arabia. A man at once a fighter and a Saint and with the adventurous recklessness of a boy. In the years that had succeeded the war of 1939-1945, Europe and the East had undergone a black period. Fear had been in the ascendant, and Fear had bred its new crop of cruelties and savageries. Civilization had begun to crack. In India and Persia abominable things had happened; wholesale massacres, famines, tortures, anarchy. . . .

And through the black mist a figure, an almost legendary figure had appeared—the man calling himself "Father Clement"—saving children, rescuing people from torture, leading his flock by impassable ways over mountains, bringing them to safe zones, settling them in communities. Worshipped, loved, adored—a legend, not a man.

And according to Catherine Yougoubian, Father Clement was John Gabriel, former M.P. for St. Loo, womanizer, drunkard; the man who first, last, and all the time, played for his own hand. An adventurer, an opportunist, a man with no virtues save the virtue of physical courage.

Suddenly, uneasily, my incredulity wavered. Impossible as I believed Catherine's tale to be, there was one point of plausibility. Both Father Clement and John Gabriel were men of unusual physical courage. Some of those exploits of the legendary figure, the audacity of the rescues, the sheer bluff, the—yes, the impudence of his methods, were John Gabriel's methods all right.

But John Gabriel had always been a self advertiser. Everything he did, he did with an eye on the gallery. If John Gabriel was Father Clement, the whole world would surely have been advised of the fact.

No, I didn't—I couldn't—believe. . . .

But when Catherine stopped breathless, when the fire in her eyes died down, when she said in her old persistent monotonous manner, "You will come now, yes, please?" I shouted for Parfitt.

He helped me up and gave me my crutches and assisted me down the stairs and into a taxi, and Catherine got in beside me.

I had to know, you see. Curiosity, perhaps? Or the persistence of Catherine Yougoubian? (I should certainly have had to give way to her in the end!) Anyway, I wanted to see John Gabriel. I wanted to see if I could reconcile the Father Clement story with what I knew of the John Gabriel of St. Loo. I wanted, perhaps, to see if I could see what Isabella had seen—what she must have seen to have done as she had done. . . .

I don't know what I expected as I followed Catherine Yougoubian up the narrow stairs and into the little back bedroom. There was a French doctor there, with a beard and a pontifical manner. He was bending over his patient, but he drew back and motioned me forward courteously.

I noticed his eyes appraising me curiously. I was the person that a great man, dying, had expressed a wish to see. . . .

I had a shock when I saw Gabriel. It was so long since that day in Zagrade. I would not have recognized the figure that lay so quietly on the bed. He was dying, I saw that. The end was very near now. And it seemed to me that I recognized nothing I knew in the face of the man lying there. For I had to acknowledge that, as far as appearances went, Catherine had been right. That emaciated face was the face of a Saint. It had the marks of suffering, of agony. . . . It had the asceticism. And it had, finally, the spiritual peace. . . .

And none of these qualities had anything to do with the man whom I had known as John Gabriel.

Then he opened his eyes and saw me—and he grinned. It was the same grin, the same eyes—beautiful eyes in a small ugly clown's face.

His voice was very weak. He said, "So she got you! Armenians are wonderful!"

Yes, it was John Gabriel. He motioned to the doctor. He demanded in his weak suffering imperious voice, a promised stimulant. The doctor demurred—Gabriel overbore him. It would hasten the end, or so I guessed, but Gabriel made it clear that a last spurt of energy was important and indeed necessary to him.

The doctor shrugged his shoulders and gave in. He administered the injection and then he and Catherine left me alone with the patient.

Gabriel began at once.

"I want you to know about Isabella's death."

I told him that I knew all about that.

"No," he said, "I don't think you do . . ."

It was then that he described to me that final scene in the café in Zagrade.

I shall tell it in its proper place.

After that, he only said one thing more. It is because

of that one thing more that I am writing this story.

Father Clement belongs to history. His incredible life of heroism, endurance, compassion, and courage belongs to those people who like writing the lives of heroes. The communities he started are the foundation of our new tentative experiments in living, and there will be many biographies of the man who imagined and created them.

This is not the story of Father Clement. It is the story of John Merryweather Gabriel, a V.C. in the war, an opportunist, a man of sensual passions and of great personal charm. He and I, in our different way, loved the same woman.

We all start out as the central figure of our own story. Later we wonder, doubt, get confused. So it has been with me. First it was *my* story. Then I thought it was Jennifer and I together—Romeo and Juliet, Tristan and Iseult. And then, in my darkness and disillusionment, Isabella sailed across my vision like the moon on a dark night. She became the central theme of the embroidery, and I—I was the cross-stitch background—no more. No more, but also no less, for without the drab background, the pattern will not stand out.

Now, again, the pattern has shifted. This is not my story, not Isabella's story. It is the story of John Gabriel.

The story ends here, where I am beginning it. It ends with John Gabriel. But it also begins here.

CHAPTER ONE

Where to begin? At St. Loo? At the meeting in the Memorial Hall when the prospective Conservative candidate, Major John Gabriel, V.C., was introduced by an old (a very old) General, and stood there and made his speech, disappointing us all a little by his flat common voice and his ugly face, so that we had to fortify ourselves by the recollection of his gallantry and by reminding ourselves that it was necessary to get into touch with the People— the privileged classes were now so pitifully small!

Or shall I begin at Polnorth House, in the long low room that faced the sea, with the terrace outside where my invalid couch could be drawn out on fine days and I could look out to the Atlantic with its thundering breakers, and the dark gray rocky point which broke the line of the horizon and on which rose the battlements and the turrets of St. Loo Castle—looking, as I always felt, like a water color sketch done by a romantic young lady in the year 1860 or thereabouts.

For St. Loo Castle has that bogus, that phony air of theatricality, of spurious romance which can only be given by something that is in fact genuine. It was built, you see, when human nature was unself-conscious enough to enjoy romanticism without feeling ashamed of it. It suggests sieges, and dragons, and captive princesses and knights in armor, and all the pageantry of a rather bad historical film. And of course when you come to think of it, a bad film is exactly what history really is.

When you looked at St. Loo Castle, you expected something like Lady St. Loo, and Lady Tressilian, and Mrs. Bigham Charteris, and Isabella. The shock was that you got them!

Shall I begin there, with the visit paid by those three old ladies with their erect bearing, their dowdy clothing, their diamonds in old-fashioned settings? With my saying to Teresa in a fascinated voice, "But they can't—they simply can't—be *real?*"

Or shall I start a little earlier; at the moment, for instance, when I got into the car and started for Northolt Aerodrome to meet Jennifer . . . ?

But behind that again is *my* life—which had started thirty-eight years before and which came to an end that day. . . .

This is not *my* story. I have said that before. But it began as my story. It began with me, Hugh Norreys. Looking back over my life, I see that it has been a life much like any other man's life. Neither more interesting, nor less so. It has had the inevitable disillusionments and disappointments, the secret childish agonies; it has had also the excitements, the harmonies, the intense satisfactions arising from oddly inadequate causes. I can choose from which angle I will view my life—from the angle of frustration, or as a triumphant chronicle. Both are true. It is, in the end, always a question of selection. There is Hugh Norreys as he sees himself, and Hugh Norreys as he appears to others. There must actually be, too, Hugh Norreys as he appears to God. There must be the essential Hugh. But his story is the story that only the recording angel can write. It comes back to this: How much do I know, now, of the young man who got into the train at Penzance in the early days of 1945 on his way to London? Life had, I should have said if asked, on the whole treated me well. I liked my peacetime job of schoolmastering. I had enjoyed my war experiences—I had my job waiting to return to—and the prospect of a partnership and a headmastership in the future. I had had love affairs that had hurt me, and I had had love affairs that had satisfied me, but none that went deep. I had family ties that were adequate, but not too close. I was thirty-seven and on that particular day I was conscious of something of which I had been half-conscious for some time. I was waiting for something . . . for an experience, for a supreme event. . . .

Everything up to then in my life, I suddenly felt, had been superficial—I was waiting now for something *real.* Probably everyone experiences such a feeling once at least in their lives. Sometimes it comes early, sometimes late. It is a moment that corresponds to the moment in a cricket match when you go in to bat. . . .

I got on the train at Penzance and I took a ticket for third lunch (because I had just finished a rather large breakfast) and when the attendant came along the train shouting out nasally, "Third lunch, please, tickets ooon-lee . . ." I got up and went along to the dining car and the attendant took my ticket and gestured me into a single seat, back to the engine, opposite the place where Jennifer was sitting.

That, you see, is how things happen. You cannot take thought for them, you cannot plan. I sat down opposite Jennifer—and Jennifer was crying.

I didn't see it at first. She was struggling hard for control. There was no sound, no outward indication. We did not look at each other, we behaved with due regard to the conventions governing the meeting of strangers on a restaurant car. I advanced the menu towards her—a polite but meaningless action since it only bore the legend: Soup, Fish or Meat, Sweet or Cheese. 4/6.

She accepted my gesture with the answering gesture, a polite ritualistic smile and an inclination of the head. The attendant asked us what we would have to drink. We both had light ale.

Then there was a pause. I looked at the magazine I had brought in with me. The attendant dashed along the car with plates of soup and set them in front of us. Still the little gentleman, I advanced the salt and pepper an inch in Jennifer's direction. Up to now I had not looked at her —not really looked, that is to say—though of course I knew certain basic facts. That she was young, but not very young, a few years younger than myself, that she was of medium height and dark, that she was of my own social standing and that while attractive enough to be pleasant, she was not so overwhelmingly attractive as to be in any sense disturbing.

Presently I intended to look rather more closely, and if it seemed indicated I should probably advance a few tentative remarks. It would depend.

But the thing that suddenly upset all my calculations was the fact that my eyes, straying over the soup plate opposite me, noticed that something unexpected was splashing into the soup. Without noise, or sound, or any indication of distress, tears were forcing themselves from her eyes and dropping into the soup.

I was startled. I cast swift surreptitious glances at her. The tears soon stopped, she succeeded in forcing them back, she drank her soup. I said, quite unpardonably, but irresistibly:

"You're dreadfully unhappy, aren't you?"

And she replied fiercely, "I'm a perfect fool!"

Neither of us spoke. The waiter took the soup plates away. He laid minute portions of meat pie in front of us and helped us from a monstrous dish of cabbage. To this he added two roast potatoes with the air of one doing us a special favor.

I looked out of the window and made a remark about the scenery. I proceeded to a few remarks about Cornwall. I said I didn't know it well. Did she? She said, Yes, she did, she lived there. We compared Cornwall with Devonshire, and with Wales, and with the East coast. None of our conversation meant anything. It served the purpose of glossing over the fact that she had been guilty of shedding tears in a public place and that I had been guilty of noticing the fact.

It was not until we had coffee in front of us and I had offered her a cigarette and she had accepted it, that we got back to where we had started.

I said I was sorry I had been so stupid, but that I couldn't help it. She said I must have thought her a perfect idiot.

"No," I said. "I thought that you'd come to the end of your tether. That was it, wasn't it?"

She said, Yes, that was it.

"It's humiliating," she said fiercely, "to get to such a pitch of self-pity that you don't care what you do or who sees you!"

"But you *did* care. You were struggling hard."

"I didn't actually howl," she said, "if that's what you mean."

I asked her how bad it was?

She said it was pretty bad. She had got to the end of everything, and she didn't know what to do.

I think I had already sensed that. There was an air of taut desperation about her. I wasn't going to let her get away from me while she was in that mood. I said, "Come on, tell me about it. I'm a stranger—you can say things to a stranger. It won't matter."

She said, "There's nothing to tell except that I've made the most bloody mess of everything—*everything*."

I told her it wasn't probably as bad as all that. She needed, I could see, reassurance. She needed new life, new courage—she needed lifting up from a pitiful slough of endurance and suffering and setting on her feet again. I had not the slightest doubt that I was the person best qualified to do that. . . . Yes, it happened as soon as that.

She looked at me doubtfully, like an uncertain child. Then she poured it all out.

In the midst of it, of course, the attendant came with the bill. I was glad then that we were having the third lunch. They wouldn't hustle us out of the dining car. I added ten shillings to my bill, and the attendant bowed discreetly and melted away.

I went on listening to Jennifer.

She'd had a raw deal. She'd stood up to things with an incredible amount of pluck, but there had been too many things, one after the other, and she wasn't, physically, strong. Things had gone wrong for her all along—as a child, as a girl, in her marriage. Her sweetness, her impulsiveness, had landed her every time in a hole. There had been loopholes for escape and she hadn't taken them—she'd preferred to try and make the best of a bad job. And when that had failed, and a loophole had presented itself, it had been a bad loophole, and she'd landed herself in a worse mess than ever.

For everything that had happened, she blamed herself. My heart warmed to that lovable trait in her—there was no judgment, no resentment. "It must," she ended up wistfully every time, "have been my fault somehow . . ."

I wanted to roar out, "Of course it wasn't your fault! Don't you see that you're a victim—that you'll always be a victim—so long as you adopt that fatal attitude of being willing to take all the blame for everything?"

She was adorable sitting there, worried and miserable and defeated. I think I knew then, looking at her across the narrow table, what it was I had been waiting for. It was Jennifer . . . not Jennifer as a possession, but to give Jen-

nifer back her mastery of life, to see Jennifer happy, to see
her *whole* once more.

Yes, I knew then . . . though it wasn't until many weeks
afterwards that I admitted to myself that I was in love
with her.

You see, there was so much more to it than that.

We made no plans for meeting again. I think she believed truly that we would not meet again. I knew otherwise. She had told me her name. She said, very sweetly,
when we at last left the dining car, "This is goodbye. But
please believe I shall never forget you and what you've
done for me. I was desperate—quite desperate."

I took her hand and I said goodbye—but I knew it
wasn't goodbye. I was so sure of it that I would have been
willing to agree not even to try and find her again. But as it
chanced there were friends of hers who were friends of
mine. I did not tell her, but to find her again would be
easy. What was odd was that we had not happened to meet
before this.

I met her again a week later, at Caro Strangeways' cocktail party. And after that, there was no more doubt about
it. We both knew what had happened to us. . . .

We met and parted and met again. We met at parties,
in other people's houses, we met at small quiet restaurants,
we took trains into the country and walked together in a
world that was all a shining haze of unreal bliss. We went
to a concert and heard Elizabeth Schumann sing "And in
that pathway where our feet shall wander, we'll meet, forget the earth and lost in dreaming, bid heaven unite a love
that earth no more shall sunder . . ."

And as we went out into the noise and bustle of Wig-
more Street I repeated the last words of Strauss' song "—in
love and bliss ne'er ending . . ." and met her eyes.

She said, "Oh no, not for us, Hugh . . . "

And I said, "Yes, for us. . . ."

Because, as I pointed out to her, we had got to go
through the rest of our lives together. . . .

She couldn't, she said, throw everything over like that.
Her husband, she knew, wouldn't consent to let her divorce
him.

"But he'd divorce you?"

"Yes, I suppose so . . . Oh Hugh, can't we go on as we are?"

No, I said, we couldn't. I'd been waiting, watching her fight her way back to health and sanity. I hadn't wanted to let her vex herself with decisions until she was once more the happy joyful creature Nature had created her to be. Well, I'd done it. She was strong again—strong mentally and physically. And we'd got to come to a decision.

It wasn't plain sailing. She had all sorts of queer, quite unpredictable objections. Chiefly, it was because of me and my career that she demurred. It would mean a complete breakup for me. Yes, I said, I knew that. I'd thought it out, and it didn't matter. I was young—there were other things that I could do besides schoolmastering.

She cried then and said that she'd never forgive herself if, because of her, I were to ruin my life. I told her that nothing could ruin it, unless she herself were to leave me. Without her, I said, life would be finished for me.

We had a lot of ups and downs. She would seem to accept my view, then suddenly, when I was no longer with her, she would retract. She had, you see, no confidence in herself.

Yet, little by little, she came to share my outlook. It was not only passion between us—there was more than that. That harmony of mind and thought—that delight in mind answering mind. The things that she would say—which had just been on my own lips—the sharing of a thousand small minor pleasures.

She admitted at last that I was right, that we belonged together. Her last defences went down.

"It *is* true! Oh Hugh, how it can be, I don't know. How can I really mean to you what you say I do? And yet I don't really doubt."

The thing was tested—proved. We made plans, the necessary mundane plans.

It was a cold sunny morning when I woke up and realized that on that day our new life was starting. From now on Jennifer and I would be together. Not until this moment had I allowed myself to believe fully. I had always feared that her strange morbid distrust of her own capabilities would make her draw back.

Even on this, the last morning of the old life, I had to make quite sure. I rang her up.

"Jennifer . . ."

"Hugh . . ."

Her voice, soft with a tiny tremor in it . . . It was true. I said:

"Forgive me, darling. I had to hear your voice. Is it all true?"

"It's all true. . . ."

We were to meet at Northolt Aerodrome. I hummed as I dressed, I shaved carefully. In the mirror I saw a face almost unrecognizable with sheer idiotic happiness. This was *my* day! The day I had waited for for thirty-eight years. I breakfasted, checked over tickets, passport. I went down to the car. Harriman was driving. I told him I would drive—he could sit behind.

I turned out of the Mews into the main road. The car wound in and out of the traffic. I had plenty of time. It was a glorious morning—a lovely morning created specially for Hugh and Jennifer. I could have sung and shouted.

The lorry came at forty miles an hour out of the side road—there was no seeing or avoiding it—no failure in driving—no faulty reaction. The driver of the lorry was drunk, they told me afterwards—how little it matters *why* a thing happens!

It struck the Buick broadside on, wrecking it—pinning me under the wreckage. Harriman was killed.

Jennifer waited at the Aerodrome. The plane left . . . I did not come. . . .

CHAPTER TWO

There isn't much point in describing what came next. There wasn't, to begin with, any continuity. There was confusion, darkness, pain. . . . I wandered endlessly, it seemed to me, in long underground corridors. At intervals I realized dimly that I was in a hospital ward. I was aware of doctors, white-capped nurses, the smell of antiseptics— the flashing of steel instruments, glittering little glass trolleys being wheeled briskly about. . . .

Realization came to me slowly—there was less confusion, less pain . . . but no thoughts as yet of people or of places. The animal in pain knows only pain or the surcease of pain, it can concentrate on nothing else. Drugs, mercifully dulling physical suffering, confuse the mind; heightening the impression of chaos.

But lucid intervals began to come—there was the moment when they told me definitely that I had had an accident.

Knowledge came at last—knowledge of my helplessness—of my wrecked broken body. . . . There was no more life for me as a man amongst men.

People came to see me—my brother, awkward, tongue-tied, with no idea of what to say. We had never been very close. I could not speak to him of Jennifer.

But it was of Jennifer I was thinking. As I improved, they brought me my letters. Letters from Jennifer . . .

Only my immediate family had been admitted to see me. Jennifer had had no claim, no right. She had been technically only a friend.

They won't let me come, Hugh darling, she wrote. *I shall come as soon as they do. All my love. Concentrate on getting better, Jennifer.*

And another:

Don't worry, Hugh. Nothing matters so long as you are not dead. That's all that matters. We shall be together soon—for always. Yours Jennifer.

I wrote to her, a feeble pencil scrawl, that she mustn't come. What had I to offer Jennifer now?

It was not until I was out of the hospital and in my brother's house that I saw Jennifer again. Her letters had all sounded the same note. We loved each other! Even if I never recovered we must be together. She would look after me. There would still be happiness—not the happiness of which we had once dreamed, but still happiness.

And though my first reaction had been to cut the knot ruthlessly, to say to Jennifer, "Go away, and never come near me," I wavered. Because I believed, as she did, that the tie between us was not of the flesh only. All the·delights of mental companionship would still be ours. Certainly it would be best for her to go and forget me—but if she would not go?

It was a long time before I gave in and let her come. We wrote to each other frequently and those letters of ours were true love letters. They were inspiring—heroic in tone—

And so, at last, I let her come. . . .

Well, she came.

She wasn't allowed to stay very long. We knew then, I suppose—but we wouldn't admit it. She came again. She came a third time. After that, I simply couldn't stand it any longer. Her third visit lasted ten minutes, and it seemed like an hour and a half! I could hardly believe it when I looked at my watch afterwards. It had seemed, I have no doubt, just as long to her. . . .

For you see we had nothing to say to each other. . . .

Yes, just that. . . .

There wasn't, after all, anything there.

Is there any bitterness like the bitterness of a fool's paradise? All that communion of mind with mind, our thoughts that leapt to complete each other, our friendship, our companionship: illusion—nothing but illusion. The illusion that mutual attraction between man and woman breeds. Nature's lure, Nature's last and most cunning piece of deceit. Between me and Jennifer there had been the attraction of the flesh only—from that had sprung the whole monstrous fabric of self-deception. It had been passion and passion only, and the discovery shamed me, turned me sour, brought me almost to the point of hating her as well as myself. We stared at each other desolately—wondering each in our own way what had happened to the miracle in which we had been so confident.

She was a good-looking young woman, I saw that. But when she talked she bored me. And I bored her. We couldn't talk about anything or discuss anything with any pleasure.

She kept reproaching herself for the whole thing, and I wished she wouldn't. It seemed unnecessary and just a trifle hysterical. I thought to myself, Why on earth has she got to fuss so?

As she left the third time she said, in her persevering bright way, "I'll come again very soon, Hugh darling."

"No," I said. "Don't come."

"But of course I shall." Her voice was hollow, insincere.

I said savagely, "For God's sake don't pretend, Jennifer. It's finished—it's all finished."

She said it wasn't finished, that she didn't know what I meant. She was going to spend her life looking after me, she said, and we would be very happy. She was determined on self-immolation, and it made me see red. I felt apprehensive, too, that she would do as she said. Perhaps she would always be there, chattering, trying to be kind, uttering foolish bright remarks . . . I got in a panic—a panic born of weakness and illness.

I yelled at her to go away—go *away*. She went, looking frightened. But I saw relief in her eyes.

When my sister-in-law came in later to draw the curtains, I spoke. I said, "It's over, Teresa. She's gone . . . she's gone . . . She won't come back, will she?"

Teresa said in her quiet voice, No, she wouldn't come back.

"Do you think, Teresa," I asked, "that it's my illness that makes me see things—wrong?"

Teresa knew what I meant. She said that, in her opinion, an illness like mine tended to make you see things as they really were.

"You mean that I'm seeing Jennifer now as she really is?"

Teresa said she didn't mean quite that. I wasn't probably any better able to know what Jennifer was really like now than before. But I knew now exactly what effect Jennifer produced on *me*, apart from my being in love with her.

I asked her what she herself thought of Jennifer.

She said that she had always thought Jennifer was attractive, nice, and not at all interesting.

"Do you think she's very unhappy, Teresa?" I asked morbidly.

"Yes, Hugh, I do."

"Because of me?"

"No, because of herself."

I said, "She goes on blaming herself for my accident. She keeps saying that if I hadn't been coming to meet *her*, it would never have happened—it's all so *stupid!*"

"It is, rather."

"I don't want her to work herself up about it. I don't want her to be unhappy, Teresa."

"Really, Hugh," said Teresa. "Do leave the girl something!"

"What do you mean?"

"She *likes* being unhappy. Haven't you realized that?"

There is a cold clarity about my sister-in-law's thought processes that I find very disconcerting.

I told her that that was a beastly thing to say.

Teresa said thoughtfully that perhaps it was, but that she hadn't really thought it mattered saying so now.

"You haven't got to tell yourself fairy stories any longer. Jennifer has always loved sitting down and thinking how everything has gone wrong. She broods over it and works herself up—but if she likes living that way, why shouldn't she?" Teresa added, "You know, Hugh, you can't feel pity for a person unless there's self-pity there. A person has to be sorry for themselves before you can be sorry for them. Pity has always been your weakness. Because of it you don't see things clearly."

I found momentary satisfaction in telling Teresa that she was an odious woman. She said she thought she probably was.

"You are never sorry for anyone."

"Yes, I am. I'm sorry for Jennifer in a way."

"And me?"

"I don't know, Hugh."

I said sarcastically:

"The fact that I'm a maimed broken wreck with nothing to live for doesn't affect you at all?"

"I don't know if I'm sorry for you or not. This means that you're going to start your life all over again, living it from an entirely different angle. That might be very interesting."

I told Teresa that she was inhuman, and she went away smiling.

She had done me a lot of good.

CHAPTER THREE

It was soon afterwards that we moved to St. Loo in Cornwall.

Teresa had just inherited a house there from a great-aunt. The doctor wanted me to be out of London. My brother Robert is a painter with what most people think is a perverted vision of landscapes. His war service, like most artists', had been agricultural. So it all fitted in very well.

Teresa went down and got the house ready and, having filled up a lot of forms successfully, I was borne down by special ambulance.

"What goes on here?" I asked Teresa on the morning after my arrival.

Teresa was well-informed. There were, she said, three separate worlds. There was the old fishing village, grouped round its harbor, with the tall slate-roofed houses rising up all round it, and the notices written in Flemish and French as well as English. Beyond that, sprawling out along the coast, was the modern tourist and residential excrescence. The large luxury hotels, thousands of small bungalows, masses of little boarding houses—all very busy and active in summer, quiet in winter. Thirdly, there was St. Loo Castle, ruled over by the old dowager, Lady St. Loo, a nucleus of yet another way of life with ramifications stretching up through winding lanes to houses tucked inconspicuously away in valleys beside old world churches. County, in fact, said Teresa.

"And what are we?" I asked.

Teresa said we were "county" too, because Polnorth House had belonged to her great-aunt Miss Amy Tregellis, and it was hers, Teresa's, by inheritance and not by purchase, so that we belonged.

"Even Robert?" I asked. "In spite of his being a painter?"

That, Teresa admitted, would take a little swallowing. There were too many painters at St. Loo in the summer months.

"But he's my husband," said Teresa superbly, "and besides, his mother was a Bolduro from Bodmin way."

It was then that I invited Teresa to tell us what we were going to do in the new home—or rather what she was going to do. My rôle was clear. I was the looker-on.

Teresa said she was going to participate in all the local goings-on.

"Which are?"

Teresa said she thought mainly politics and gardening, with a dash of Women's Institutes and good causes such as Welcoming the Soldiers Home.

"But principally politics," she said. "After all, a General Election will be on us any minute."

"Have you ever taken any interest in politics, Teresa?"

"No, Hugh, I haven't. It has always seemed to me unnecessary. I have confined myself to voting for the candidate who seems to me likely to do least harm."

"An admirable policy," I murmured.

But now, Teresa said, she would do her best to take politics seriously. She would have, of course, to be a Conservative. Nobody who owned Polnorth House could be anything else, and the late Miss Amy Tregellis would turn in her grave if the niece to whom she had bequeathed her treasures was to vote Labour.

"But if you believe Labour to be the better party?"

"I don't," said Teresa. "I don't think there's anything to choose between them."

"Nothing could be fairer than that," I said.

When we had been settled in at Polnorth House a fortnight, Lady St. Loo came to call upon us.

She brought with her her sister, Lady Tressilian, her sister-in-law, Mrs. Bigham Charteris, and her granddaughter, Isabella.

After they had left, I said in a fascinated voice to Teresa that they couldn't be real.

They were, you see, so exactly right to have come out of St. Loo Castle. They were pure fairy story. The Three Witches and the Enchanted Maiden.

Adelaide St. Loo was the widow of the seventh Baron. Her husband had been killed in the Boer War. Her two sons had been killed in the war of 1914-1918. They left behind them no sons, but the younger left a daughter, Isabella, whose mother had died at her birth. The title passed to a cousin, then resident in New Zealand. The ninth Lord St. Loo was only too pleased to rent the Castle to the old dowager. Isabella was brought up there, watched over by her guardians, her grandmother and her two great-aunts. Lady St. Loo's widowed sister, Lady Tressilian, and her widowed sister-in-law, Mrs. Bigham Charteris, came to join her. They shared expenses and so made it possible for Isabella to be brought up in what the old ladies considered her rightful home. They were all over seventy, and had somewhat the appearance of three black crows. Lady St. Loo had a vast bony face, with an eagle nose and a high forehead. Lady Tressilian was plump and had a large round face with little twinkling eyes. Mrs. Bigham Charteris was lean and leathery. They achieved in their appearance a kind of Edwardian effect—as though time had stood still for them. They wore jewelry, rather dirty, indubitably real, pinned on them in unlikely places—not too much of it. It was usually in the form of crescents or horseshoes or stars.

Such were the three old ladies of St. Loo Castle. With them came Isabella—a very fair representative of an enchanted maiden. She was tall and thin, and her face was long and thin with a high forehead, and straight falling ash-blond hair. She was almost incredibly like a figure out of an early stained-glass window. She could not have been

called actually pretty, nor attractive, but there was about
her something that you might almost call beauty—only it
was the beauty of a time long past—it was most definitely
not at all the modern idea of beauty. There was no anima-
tion in her, no charm of coloring, no irregularity of feature.
Her beauty was the severe beauty of good structure—good
bone formation. She looked medieval, severe and austere.
But her face was not characterless; it had what I can only
describe as nobility.

After I had said to Teresa that the old ladies weren't
real, I added that the girl wasn't real either.

"The Princess imprisoned in the ruined castle?" Teresa suggested.

"Exactly. She ought to have come here on a milk white
steed and not in a very old Daimler." I added with curiosity, "I wonder what she thinks about."

For Isabella had said very little during the official visit.
She had sat very upright, with a sweet rather faraway
smile. She had responded politely to any conversational
overtures made to her, but there had not been much need
for her to sustain the conversation since her grandmother
and aunts had monopolized most of the talk. I wondered
if she had been bored to come, or interested in something
new turning up in St. Loo. Her life, I thought, must be
rather dull.

I asked curiously, "Didn't she get called up at all during the war? Did she stay at home through it all?"

"She's only nineteen. She's been driving for the Red
Cross here since she left school."

"School?" I was astonished. "Do you mean she's been
to school? Boarding school?"

"Yes. St. Ninian's."

I was even more surprised. For St. Ninian's is an expensive and up-to-date school—not co-educational, or in
any sense a crank school—but an establishment priding itself on its modern outlook. Not in any sense a fashionable
finishing school.

"Do you find that astonishing?" Teresa asked.

"Yes, do you know, I do," I said slowly. "That girl
gives you the impression that she's never been away from

home, that she's been brought up in some bygone medieval environment that is completely out of touch with the twentieth century."

Teresa nodded her head thoughtfully. "Yes," she said. "I know what you mean."

My brother Robert chimed in here. It just showed, he said, how the only environment that counted was home environment—that and hereditary disposition.

"I still wonder," I said curiously, "what she thinks about . . ."

"Perhaps," said Teresa, "she doesn't think."

I laughed at Teresa's suggestion. But I wondered still in my own mind about this curious stick of a girl.

At that particular time I was suffering from an almost morbid self-consciousness about my own condition. I had always been a healthy and athletic person—I had disliked such things as illness or deformity, or ever having my attention called to them. I had been capable of pity, yes, but with pity had always gone a faint repulsion.

And now I was an object to inspire pity and repulsion. An invalid, a cripple, a man lying on a couch with twisted limbs—a rug pulled up over him.

And sensitively I waited, shrinking, for everyone's reaction to my state. Whatever it was, it invariably made me flinch. The kindly commiserating glance was horrible to me. No less horrible was the obvious tact that managed to pretend that I was an entirely natural object, that the visitor hadn't noticed anything unusual. But for Teresa's iron will, I would have shut myself up and seen nobody at all. But Teresa, when she is determined on anything, is not easy to withstand. She was determined that I should not become a recluse. She managed, without the aid of the spoken word, to suggest that to shut myself up and make a mystery of myself would be a form of self-advertisement. I knew what she was doing and why she was doing it, but nevertheless I responded. Grimly I set out to show her I could take it—no matter what it was! Sympathy, tact, the extra kindliness in a voice, the conscientious avoidance of any reference to accidents or illness, the pretence that I was as other men—I endured them all with a poker face.

I had not found the old ladies' reaction to my state too embarrassing. Lady St. Loo had adopted the line of tactful avoidance. Lady Tressilian, a maternal type, had not been able to help exuding maternal compassion. She had stressed, rather obviously, the latest books. She wondered if, perhaps, I did any reviewing? Mrs. Bigham Charteris, a blunter type, had shown her awareness only by rather obviously checking herself when speaking of the more active blood sports. (Poor devil, mustn't mention hunting or the beagles.)

Only the girl, Isabella, had surprised me by being natural. She had looked at me without any suggestion of having to look away quickly. She had looked at me as though her mind registered me along with the other occupants of the room and with the furniture. *One man, age over thirty, broken.* . . . An item in a catalogue—a catalogue of things that had nothing to do with her.

When she had finished with me, her eyes went on to the grand piano, and then to Robert and Teresa's Tang Horse which stood on a table by itself. The Tang Horse seemed to awaken a certain amount of interest in her. She asked me what it was. I told her.

"Do you like it?" I asked her.

She considered quite carefully before replying. Then she said—and gave the monosyllable a lot of weight, as though it was important—"Yes."

I wondered if she was a moron.

I asked her if she was fond of horses.

She said this was the first one she'd seen.

"No," I said, "I meant real horses."

"Oh, I see. Yes, I am. But I can't afford to hunt."

"Would you like to hunt?"

"Not particularly. There's not very much good country round here."

I asked her if she sailed and she said she did. Then Lady Tressilian began talking to me about books, and Isabella relapsed into silence. She had, I noticed then, one art highly developed; the art of repose. She could sit still. She didn't smoke, she didn't cross her legs, or swing them, or fiddle with her hands, or pat her hair. She sat quite still and upright in the tall grandfather chair, with her hands on her lap—long narrow hands. She was as immobile as the Tang Horse—it on its table, she in her chair. They had something, I thought, of the same quality—highly decorative—static—belonging to a bygone age. . . .

I laughed when Teresa suggested that she didn't think, but later it occurred to me that it might be true. Animals don't think—their minds are relaxed, passive, until an emergency arises with which they have to deal. Thinking (in the speculative sense of the word) is really a highly artificial process which we have taught ourselves with some trouble. We worry over what we did yesterday, and debate what we are going to do today and what will happen to-morrow. But yesterday, today and tomorrow exist quite independently of our speculation. They have happened and will happen to us no matter what we do about it.

Teresa's prognostications of our life at St. Loo were singularly accurate. Almost at once we became plunged up to the neck in politics. Polnorth House was large and rambling, and Miss Amy Tregellis, her income diminished by taxation, had shut off a wing of it, providing this with a separate kitchen. It had been done originally for evacuees from the bombed areas. But the evacuees, arriving from London in mid-winter, had been unable to stomach the horrors of Polnorth House. In St. Loo itself, with its shops and its bungalows, they might have been able to support life, but a mile from the town, along "that narsty winding lane—the mud, yer wouldn't believe it—and no lights—and anybody might jump out on yer from be'ind the hedge. And vegetables all mud out of the garden, too much green stuff, and milk—coming right from a cow—quite hot sometimes—disgusting—and never a tin of condensed handy!" It was too much for Mrs. Price and Mrs. Hardy and their offspring. They departed secretly at early dawn taking their broods back to the dangers of London. They were nice women. They left the place clean and scrubbed and a note on the table.

"Thanking you, Miss, for your kindness, and we know you've done all you can, but it's just too awful in the country, and the children having to walk in the mud to school.

But thanking you all the same. I hope as everything has been left all right."

The billeting officer did not try any more. He was learning wisdom. In due course Miss Tregellis let the detached wing to Captain Carslake, the Conservative agent, who also led a busy life as an Air Raid Warden and an officer in the Home Guard.

Robert and Teresa were perfectly willing for the Carslakes to continue as tenants. Indeed, it was doubtful if they could have turned them out. But it meant that a great deal of pre-election activity centred in and around Polnorth House as well as the Conservative offices in St. Loo High Street.

Teresa, as she had foreseen, was swept into the vortex. She drove cars, and distributed leaflets, and did a little tentative canvassing. St. Loo's recent political history was unsettled. As a fashionable seaside watering place, superimposed on a fishing port, and with agricultural surroundings, it had naturally always returned a Conservative. The outlying agricultural districts were Conservative to a man. But the character of St. Loo had changed in the last fifteen years. It had become a tourist resort in summer with small boarding houses. It had a large colony of artists' bungalows, like a rash, spread along the cliffs. The people who made up the present population were serious, artistic, cultured and, in politics, definitely pink if not red.

There had been a by-election in 1943 on the retirement of Sir George Borrodaile at the age of sixty-nine after his second stroke. And to the horror of the old inhabitants, for the first time in history, a Labour M.P. was returned.

"Mind you," said Captain Carslake, swaying to and fro on his heels as he imparted past history to Teresa and myself, "I'm not saying we didn't ask for it."

Carslake was a lean little dark man, horsy-looking, with sharp almost furtive eyes. He had become a captain in 1918 when he had entered the Army Service Corps. He was competent politically and knew his job.

You must understand that I myself am a tyro in politics—I never really understand the jargon. My account of the St. Loo election is probably wildly inaccurate. It bears the same relation to reality as Robert's pictures of trees do to the particular trees he happens to be painting at the moment. The actual trees are trees, entities with barks and branches and leaves and acorns or chestnuts. Robert's trees are blodges and splodges of thick oil paint applied in a certain pattern and wildly surprising colors to a certain area of canvas. The two things are not at all alike. In my own opinion, Robert's trees are not even recognizable as trees—they might just as easily be plates of spinach or a gas works. But they are Robert's *idea* of trees. And my account of politics in St. Loo is my impression of a political election. It is probably not recognizable as such to a politician. I daresay I shall get the terms and the procedure wrong. But to me the election was only the unimportant and confusing background for a life-size figure—John Gabriel.

CHAPTER FOUR

The first mention of John Gabriel came on the evening when Carslake was explaining to Teresa that as regards the results of the by-election they had asked for it.

Sir James Bradwell of Torington Park had been the Conservative candidate. He was a resident of the district, he had some money, and was a good dyed-in-the-wool Tory with sound principles. He was a man of upright character. He was also sixty-two, devoid of intellectual fire, or of quick reactions—had no gift of public speaking and was quite helpless if heckled.

"Pitiful on a platform," said Carslake. "Quite pitiful. Er and ah and erhem—just couldn't get on with it. We wrote his speeches, of course, and we had a good speaker down always for the important meetings. It would have been all right ten years ago. Good honest chap, local, straight as a die, and a gentleman. But nowadays—they want more than that!"

"They want brains?" I suggested.

Carslake didn't seem to think much of brains.

"They want a downy sort of chap—slick—knows the answers, can get a quick laugh. And, of course, they want someone who'll promise the earth. An old-fashioned chap like Bradwell is too conscientious to do that sort of thing. He won't say that everyone will have houses, and the war will end tomorrow, and every woman's going to have central heating and a washing machine.

"And of course," he went on, "the swing of the pendulum had begun. We've been in too long. Anything for a change. The other chap, Wilbraham, was a competent fellow, earnest, been a schoolmaster, invalided out of the Army, big talk about what was going to be done for the returning ex-serviceman—and the usual hot air about Nationalisation and the Health Schemes. What I mean is, he put over his stuff well. Got in with a majority of over two thousand. First time such a thing's ever happened in St. Loo. Shook us all up, I can tell you. We've got to do better this time. We've got to get Wilbraham out."

"Is he popular?"

"So so. Doesn't spend much money in the place, but he's conscientious and got a nice manner with him. It won't be too easy getting him out. We've got to pull our socks up all over the country."

"You don't think Labour will get in?"

We were incredulous about such a possibility before the election of 1945.

Carslake said of course Labour wouldn't get in—the county was solidly behind Churchill.

"But we shan't have the same majority in the country. Depends, of course, how the Liberal vote goes. Between you and me, Mrs. Norreys, I shan't be surprised if we see a big increase in the Liberal vote."

I glanced sideways at Teresa. She was trying to assume the face of one politically intent.

"I'm sure you'll be a great help to us," said Carslake heartily to her.

Teresa murmured, "I'm afraid I'm not a very keen politician."

Carslake said breezily, "We must all work hard."

He looked at me in a calculating manner. I at once offered to address envelopes.

"I still have the use of my arms," I said.

He looked embarrassed at once and began to rock on his heels again.

"Splendid," he said. "Splendid. Where did you get yours? North Africa?"

I said I had got it in the Harrow Road. That finished him. His embarrassment was so acute as to be catching.

Clutching at a straw, he turned to Teresa.

"Your husband," he said, "he'll help us too?"

Teresa shook her head.

"I'm afraid," she said, "he's a Communist."

If she had said Robert had been a black mamba she couldn't have upset Carslake more. He positively shuddered.

"You see," explained Teresa, "he's an artist."

Carslake brightened a little at that. Artists, writers, that sort of thing . . .

"I see," he said broad-mindedly. "Yes, I see."

"And that gets Robert out of it," Teresa said to me afterwards.

I told her that she was an unscrupulous woman.

When Robert came in, Teresa informed him of his political faith.

"But I've never been a member of the Communist party," he protested. "I mean, I do like their ideas. I think the whole ideology is right."

"Exactly," said Teresa. "That's what I told Carslake. And from time to time we'll leave Karl Marx open across the arm of your chair—and then you'll be quite safe from being asked to do anything."

"That's all very well, Teresa," said Robert doubtfully. "Suppose the other side get at me?"

Teresa reassured him.

"They won't. As far as I can see, the Labour party is far more frightened of the Communists than the Tories are."

"I wonder," I said, "what our candidate's like?"

For Carslake had been just a little evasive on the subject.

Teresa had asked him if Sir James was going to contest the seat again and Carslake had shaken his head.

"No, not this time. We've got to make a big fight. I don't know how it will go, I'm sure." He looked very harassed. "He's not a local man."

"Who is he?"

"A Major Gabriel. He's a V.C."

"This war? Or the last?"

"Oh, this war. He's quite a youngish chap. Thirty-four. Splendid war record. Got his V.C. for 'Unusual coolness, heroism and devotion to duty.' He was in command of a machine-gun position under constant enemy fire in the attack at Salerno. All but one of his crew were killed and although wounded himself he held the position alone until all the ammunition was exhausted. He then retired to the main position, killed several of the enemy with hand-grenades and dragged the remaining seriously wounded member of his crew to safety. Good show, what? Unfortunately, he's not much to look at—small insignificant chap."

"How will he stand the test of the public platform?" I asked.

Carslake's face brightened.

"Oh, he's all right there. Positively slick, if you know what I mean. Quick as lightning. Good at getting a laugh, too. Some of it, mind you, is rather cheap stuff—" For a moment Carslake's face showed a sensitive distaste. He was a real Conservative, I perceived, he preferred acute boredom to the meretriciously amusing. "But it goes down—oh yes, it goes down.

"Of course," he added, "he has no background . . ."

"You mean he isn't a Cornishman?" I said. "Where does he come from?"

"To tell you the truth, I've no idea. . . . He doesn't come from anywhere exactly—if you know what I mean. We shall keep dark on all that. Play up the war angle—gallant service—all that. He can stand, you know, for the plain man—the ordinary Englishman. He's not our usual type, of course. . . ." He looked unhappy about it. "I'm afraid Lady St. Loo doesn't really approve."

Teresa asked delicately if it mattered whether Lady St. Loo approved. It transpired that it did. Lady St. Loo was the head of the Conservative Women's Association, and the Conservative Women were a power in St. Loo. They ran things, and managed things, and got up things, and they had, so Carslake said, a great influence on the women's vote. The women's vote, he said, was always tricky.

Then he brightened up a little.

"That's one reason why I'm optimistic about Gabriel," he said. "He gets on with women."

"But not with Lady St. Loo?"

Lady St. Loo, Carslake said, was being very good about it. . . . She acknowledged quite frankly that she was old-fashioned. But she was whole-heartedly behind whatever the Party thought necessary.

"After all," said Carslake sadly, "times have changed. We used to have gentlemen in politics. Precious few of them now. I wish this chap was a gentleman, but he isn't, and there it is. If you can't have a gentleman, I suppose a hero is the next best thing."

Which, I remarked to Teresa after he had left, was practically an epigram.

Teresa smiled. Then she said she was rather sorry for Major Gabriel.

"What do you think he's like?" she said. "Pretty dreadful?"

"No, I should think he was rather a nice chap."

"Because of his V.C.?"

"Lord, no. You can get a V.C. for being merely reckless —or even for being just stupid. You know, it's always said that old Freddy Elton got his V.C. for being too stupid to know when to retire from an advanced position. They called it holding on in face of almost insurmountable odds. Really he had no idea that everyone else had gone."

"Don't be ridiculous, Hugh. Why do you think this Gabriel person must be nice?"

"Simply, I think, because Carslake doesn't like him. The only man Carslake would like would be some awful stuffed shirt."

"What you mean is, that you don't like poor Captain Carslake!"

"No poor about it. Carslake fits into his job like a bug in a rug. And what a job!"

"Is it worse than any other job? It's hard work."

"Yes, that's true. But if your whole life is spent on the calculation of what effect *this* has on *that*—you'll end up by not knowing what this and that really are."

"Divorced from reality?"

"Yes, isn't that what politics really boil down to in the end? What people will believe, what they will stand, what they can be induced to think? Never plain fact."

"Ah!" said Teresa. "How right I am not to take politics seriously."

"You are always right, Teresa," I said and kissed my hand to her.

I myself didn't actually see the Conservative Candidate until the big meeting in the Drill Hall.

Teresa had procured for me an up-to-date type of wheeled invalid couch. I could be wheeled out on the terrace on it and lie there in a sheltered sunny place. Then, as the movement of the chair caused me less pain, I went further afield. I was occasionally pushed into St. Loo. The Drill Hall meeting was an afternoon one, and Teresa arranged that I should be present at it. It would, she assured me, amuse me. I replied that Teresa had curious ideas of amusement.

"You'll see," said Teresa, adding, "it will entertain you enormously to see everyone taking themselves so seriously."

"Besides," she went on, "I shall be wearing my Hat."

Teresa, who never wears a hat unless she goes to a wedding, had made an expedition to London and had returned with the kind of hat which was, according to her, suitable for a Conservative Woman.

"And what," I enquired, "is a hat suitable to a Conservative Woman?"

Teresa replied in detail.

It must, she said, be a hat of good material, not dowdy, but not too fashionable. It must set well on the head and it must not be frivolous.

She then produced the hat, and it was indeed all that Teresa had set forth that it should be.

She put it on and Robert and I applauded.

"It's damned good, Teresa," said Robert. "It makes you look earnest and as though you had a purpose in life."

You will understand, therefore, that to see Teresa sitting on the platform wearing the Hat lured me irresistibly to the Drill Hall on a remarkably fine summer's afternoon.

The Drill Hall was well filled by prosperous looking elderly people. Anybody under forty was (wisely, in my opinion) enjoying the pleasures of the seaside. As my invalid couch was carefully wheeled by a boy scout to a position of vantage near the wall by the front seats, I speculated as to the usefulness of such meetings. Everyone in this hall was sure to vote our way. Our opponents were holding an opposition meeting in the Girls' School. Presumably they, too, would have a full meeting of staunch supporters. How, then, was public opinion influenced? The loud-speaker truck? Open air meetings?

My speculations were interrupted by the shuffling of a small party of people coming onto the platform which hitherto had held nothing but chairs, a table, and a glass of water.

They whispered, gesticulated, and finally got settled in the required positions. Teresa, in the hat, was relegated to the second row amongst the minor personalities.

The Chairman, several tottery old gentlemen, the speaker from Headquarters, Lady St. Loo, two other women and the Candidate arranged themselves in the front row.

The Chairman began to speak in a quavery, rather sweet voice. His mumbled platitudes were practically inaudible. He was a very old general who had served with distinction in the Boer War. (Or was it, I queried to myself, the Crimean?) Whatever it was, it must have been a long time ago. The world he was mumbling about did not, I thought, now exist. . . . The thin, apple-sweet old voice stopped, there was spontaneous and enthusiastic applause—the applause given always, in England, to a friend who has stood the test of time. . . . Everyone in St. Loo knew old General S——. He was a fine old boy, they said, one of the old school.

With his concluding words, General S—— had introduced to the meeting a member of the new school, the Conservative Candidate, Major Gabriel, V.C.

It was then, with a deep and gusty sigh, that Lady Tressilian, whom I suddenly discovered to be in the end seat of a row close to me (I suspected that her maternal instinct had placed her there), breathed poignantly:

"It's such a pity that he's got such common legs."

I knew immediately what she meant. Yet asked to define what is or is not common in a leg, I could not for the life of me tell you. Gabriel was not a tall man. He had, I should say, the normal legs for his height—they were neither unduly long nor unduly short. His suit was quite a well cut one. Nevertheless, indubitably, those trousered legs were *not* the legs of a gentleman. Is it, perhaps, in the structure and poise of the nether limbs that the essence of gentility resides? A question for the Brains Trust.

Gabriel's face did not give him away, it was an ugly, but quite interesting face, with remarkably fine eyes. His legs gave him away every time.

He rose to his feet, smiled (an engaging smile), opened his mouth and spoke in a flat slightly cockney voice.

He spoke for twenty minutes—and he spoke well. Don't ask me what he said. Offhand I should say that he said the usual things—and said them more or less in the usual manner. But he got across. There was something dynamic about the man. You forgot what he looked like, you forgot that he had an ugly voice and accent. You had instead a great impression of earnestness—of single-minded purpose. You felt: this chap jolly well means to do his best. Sincerity—that was it, sincerity.

You felt—yes—that he *cared*. He *cared* about housing, about young couples who couldn't set up housekeeping— he *cared* about soldiers who had been overseas for many years and were due home, he *cared* about building up industrial security—about staving off unemployment. He cared, desperately, about seeing his country prosperous, because that prosperity would mean the happiness and well-doing of every small component part of that country. Every now and then, quite suddenly, he let off a squib, a flash of cheap, easily understood humor. They were quite obvious jokes—jokes that had been made many times before. They came out comfortingly because they were so familiar. But it wasn't the humor, it was his earnestness that really counted. When the war was finally over, when Japan was out of it, then would come the peace, and it would be vital then to get down to things. He, if they returned him, meant to get down to things. . . .

That was all. It was, I realized, entirely a personal performance. I don't mean that he ignored the party slogans, he didn't. He said all the correct things, spoke of the leader with due admiration and enthusiasm, mentioned the Empire. He was entirely correct. But you were being asked to support, not so much the Conservative Party Candidate as Major John Gabriel who was going to get things done, and who cared, passionately, that they should get done.

The audience liked him. They had, of course, come prepared to like him. They were Tories to a man (or woman), but I got the impression that they liked him rather more than they had thought they would. They seemed, I thought, even to wake up a little. And I said to myself, rather pleased with my idea, "Of course, the man's a dynamo!"

After the applause which was really enthusiastic, the Speaker from Headquarters was introduced. He was excellent. He said all the right things, made all the right pauses, got all the right laughs in the right places. I will confess that my attention wandered.

The meeting ended with the usual formalities.

As everyone got up and started streaming out, Lady Tressilian came and stood by me. I had been right—she was being a guardian angel. She said in her breathless, rather asthmatic voice:

"What do *you* think? Do tell me what you think?"

"He's good," I said. "Definitely he's good."

"I'm *so* glad you think so." She sighed gustily.

I wondered why my opinion should matter to her. She partially enlightened me when she said:

"I'm not as clever as Addie, you know, or Maud. I've never really studied politics—and I'm old-fashioned. I don't like the idea of M.P.s being paid, I've never got used to it. It should be a matter of serving your country—not recompensed."

"You can't always afford to serve your country, Lady Tressilian," I pointed out.

"No, I know that. Not nowadays. But it seems to me a pity. Our legislators should be drawn from the class that doesn't need to work for its living, the class that can really be indifferent to gain."

I wondered whether to say, "My dear lady, you come out of the Ark!"

But it was interesting to find a pocket of England where the old ideas still survived. The ruling class. The governing class. The upper class. All such hateful phrases. And yet—be honest—something in them?

Lady Tressilian went on:

"My father stood for Parliament, you know. He was M.P. for Garavissey for thirty years. He found it a great tax upon his time and very wearisome—but he thought it his *duty*."

My eyes strayed to the platform. Major Gabriel was talking to Lady St. Loo. His legs were definitely ill-at-ease. Did Major Gabriel think it his duty to stand for Parliament? I very much doubted it.

"I thought," said Lady Tressilian, following the direction of my eyes, "that he seemed very *sincere*. Didn't you?"

"That was how it struck me."

"And he spoke so beautifully about dear Mr. Churchill . . . I think there is no doubt at all that the country is solidly behind Mr. Churchill. Don't you agree?"

I did agree. Or rather, I thought that the Conservatives would certainly be returned to power with a small majority.

Teresa joined me and my boy scout appeared, prepared to push.

"Enjoy yourself?" I asked Teresa.

"Yes, I did."

"What do you think of our candidate?"

She did not answer until we were outside the Hall. Then she said, "I don't know."

CHAPTER FIVE

I met the candidate a couple of days later when he came over to confer with Carslake. Carslake brought him in to us for a drink.

Some question arose about clerical work done by Teresa, and she went out of the room with Carslake to clear the matter up.

I apologized to Gabriel for not being able to get up, and directed him where the drinks were, and told him to get himself one. He poured himself a pretty stiff one, I noticed.

He brought me mine, saying as he did so:

"War casualty?"

"No," I said, "Harrow Road." It was, by now, my stock answer, and I had come to derive a certain amount of amusement from the various reactions to it. Gabriel was much amused.

"Pity to say so," he remarked. "You're passing up an asset there."

"Do you expect me to invent a heroic tale?"

He said there was no need to invent anything.

"Just say, 'I was in North Africa'—or in Burma—or wherever you actually were—you have been overseas?"

I nodded. "Alamein and on."

"There you are then. Mention Alamein. That's enough —no one will ask details—they'll think they know."

"Is it worth it?"

"Well," he considered, "it's worth it with women. They love a wounded hero."

"I know that," I said with some bitterness.

He nodded with immediate comprehension.

"Yes. It must get you down sometimes. Lot of women round here. Motherly, some of them." He picked up his empty glass. "Do you mind if I have another?"

I urged him to do so.

"I'm going to dinner at the Castle," he explained. "That old bitch fairly puts the wind up me!"

We might have been Lady St. Loo's dearest friends, but I suppose he knew quite well that we weren't. John Gabriel seldom made mistakes.

"Lady St. Loo?" I asked. "Or all of them?"

"I don't mind the fat one. She's the kind you can soon get where you want them, and Mrs. Bigham Charteris is practically a horse. You've only got to neigh at her. But that St. Loo woman is the kind that can see through you and out the other side. You can't put on any fancy frills with her!

"Not that I'd try," he added.

"You know," he went on thoughtfully, "when you come up against a real aristocrat you're licked—there isn't anything you can do about it."

"I'm not sure," I said, "that I understand you."

He smiled.

"Well, in a way, you see, I'm in the wrong camp."

"You mean that you're not really a Tory in politics?"

"No, no. I mean I'm not their kind. They like, they can't help liking, the old school tie. Of course, they can't be too choosy nowadays, they've got to have blokes like me." He added meditatively, "My old man was a plumber —not a very good plumber either."

He looked at me and twinkled. I grinned back at him. In that moment I fell under his charm.

"Yes," he said, "Labour's really my ticket."

"But you don't believe in their program?" I suggested.

He said easily, "Oh, I've no beliefs. With me it's purely a matter of expediency. I've got to have a job. The war's as good as over, and the plums will soon be snapped up. I've always thought I could make a name for myself in politics. You see if I don't."

"So that's why you're a Tory? You prefer to be in the party that will be in power?"

"Good Lord," he said. "You don't think the Tories are going to get in, do you?"

I said I certainly did think so. With a reduced majority.

"Nonsense," he said. "Labour's going to sweep the country. Their majority's going to be terrific."

"But then—if you think so—"

I stopped.

"Why don't I want to be on the winning side?" He grinned. "My dear chap. That's why I'm not Labour. I don't want to be swamped in a crowd. The Opposition's the place for me. What *is* the Tory party anyway? Taken by and large it's the most muddle-headed crowd of gentlemanly inefficients combined with unbusinesslike business men. They're hopeless. They haven't got a policy, and they're all at sixes and sevens. Anyone with any ability at all will stick out a mile. You watch. I shall shoot up like a rocket!"

"If you get in," I said.

"Oh, I shall get in all right."

I looked at him curiously.

"You really think so?"

He grinned again.

"If I don't make a fool of myself. I've got my weak spots." He tossed off the remainder of his drink. "Mainly women. I must keep off women. Won't be difficult down here. Although there's a nice little number at the St. Loo Arms. Have you come across her? No," his eyes fell on my immobile state. "Sorry, of course you haven't." He was moved to add, with what seemed genuine feeling, "Hard lines."

It was the first bit of sympathy that I had not resented. It came out so naturally.

"Tell me," I said, "do you talk to Carslake like this?"

"That ass? Good Lord, no."

I have since wondered why Gabriel chose to be so frank with me that first evening. The conclusion that I have come to is that he was lonely. He was putting up a very good performance, but there was not much chance of relaxing between the acts. He knew, too, he must have known, that a crippled and immobile man always falls in the end into the rôle of the listener. I wanted entertainment. John Gabriel was quite willing to provide entertainment by taking me behind the scenes of his life. Besides, he was by nature a frank man.

I asked, with some curiosity, how Lady St. Loo behaved to him.

"Beautifully," he said. "Quite beautifully—damn her eyes! That's one of the ways she gets under my skin. There's nothing you can take hold of anywhere—there wouldn't be—she knows her stuff. These old hags—if they want to be rude they're so rude it takes your breath away —and if they don't want to be rude you can't make 'em."

I wondered a little at his vehemence. I didn't see that it could really matter to him whether an old lady like Lady St. Loo was rude to him or not. She surely didn't matter in the least. She belonged to a past era.

I said as much and he shot me a queer sideways glance.

"You wouldn't understand," he said.

"No, I don't think I do."

He said very quietly, "She thinks I'm dirt."

"My dear fellow!"

"They *look* at you—that kind. Look *through* you. You don't count. You're not there. You don't exist for them. You're just the boy with the papers, or the boy who brings the fish."

I knew then that it was Gabriel's past that was active. Some slight, some casual rudeness long ago to the plumber's son.

He took the words out of my mouth.

"Oh yes," he said. "I've got it. I'm class conscious. I hate these arrogant upper class women. They make me feel that nothing I do will ever get me there—that to them I'll always be dirt. They know all right, you see, what I really am."

I was startled. That glimpse of depths of resentment was so unexpected. There was hate there—real implacable hate. I wondered exactly what incident in the past still fermented and rankled in John Gabriel's subconscious mind.

"I know they don't count," he said. "I know their day is over. They're living, all over the country, in houses that are tumbling down, on incomes that have shrunk to practically nothing. Lots of 'em don't get enough to eat. They live off vegetables from the garden. They do their own housework as often as not. But they've got something that I can't get hold of—and never shall get hold of—some damned feeling of superiority. I'm as good as they are—in many ways I'm better, but when I'm with them I don't *feel* it."

Then he broke off with a sudden laugh.

"Don't mind me. I'm just blowing off steam." He looked out of the window. "A sham gingerbread castle—three old croaking ravens—and a girl like a stick, so stuck up she can't find a word to say to you. That's the kind of girl who felt a pea through all the mattresses, I expect."

I smiled.

"I always have thought," I said, "that the Princess and the Pea was a rather far-fetched fairy tale."

He fastened on one word.

"Princess! That's how she behaves—that's how they treat her. Like something royal out of a story book. She's not a Princess, she's an ordinary flesh and blood girl—she ought to be, anyway, with that mouth."

Teresa and Carslake came back at that moment. Presently Carslake and Gabriel departed.

"I wish he hadn't had to go," said Teresa. "I'd like to have talked to him."

"I expect," I said, "we shall see him fairly often."

She looked at me.

"You're interested," she said. "Aren't you?"

I considered.

"It's the first time," said Teresa, "the very first time that I've seen you interested in anything since we came here."

"I must be more politically minded than I thought."

"Oh," she said, "it isn't politics. It's that man."

"He's certainly a dynamic personality," I admitted. "It's a pity he's so ugly."

"I suppose he is ugly." She added thoughtfully, "He's very attractive, though."

I was quite astonished.

Teresa said: "Don't look at me like that. He *is* attractive. Any woman would tell you so."

"Well," I said, "you surprise me. I shouldn't have thought he was at all the sort of man women would have found attractive."

"You thought wrong," said Teresa.

CHAPTER SIX

On the following day, Isabella Charteris came over with a note from Lady St. Loo to Captain Carslake. I was out on the terrace in the sun. When she had delivered the note she came back along the terrace and presently sat down near me on a carved stone seat.

If she had been Lady Tressilian I should have suspected kindness to the lame dog, but Isabella was quite clearly not concerned with me at all. I have never seen anyone less so. She sat for some time quite silently. Then she said that she liked the sun.

"So do I," I said. "You're not very brown, though."

"I don't go brown."

Her skin was lovely in the clear light—it had a kind of magnolia whiteness. I noticed how proudly her head was set on. her shoulders. I could see why Gabriel had called her a Princess.

Thinking of him made me say, "Major Gabriel dined with you last night, didn't he?"

"Yes."

"Did you go to his meeting at the Drill Hall?"

"Yes."

"I didn't see you there."

"I was sitting in the second row."

"Did you enjoy it?"

She considered a moment before replying.

"No."

"Why did you go then?" I asked.

Again she thought a moment before saying, "It's one of the things we do."

I was curious.

"Do you like living down here? Are you happy?"

"Yes."

It struck me suddenly how rare it was to receive monosyllabic replies. Most people elaborate. The normal reply would be, "I love being by the sea" or "It's my home" . . . "I like the country" . . . "I love it down here." This girl contented herself with saying "Yes." But that "Yes" was curiously forceful. It really meant yes. It was a firm and definite assent. Her eyes had gone towards the Castle, and a very faint smile showed on her lips.

I knew then what she reminded me of. She was like those Acropolis Maidens of the 5th century B.C. She had that same inhuman exquisite smile. . . .

So Isabella Charteris was happy living at St. Loo Castle with three old women. Sitting here now in the sun, looking towards the Castle, she was happy. I could almost feel the quiet confident happiness that possessed her. And suddenly I was afraid—afraid for her.

I said, "Have you always been happy, Isabella?"

But I knew the answer before it came, although she considered a little before she said, "Yes."

"At school?"

"Yes."

I could not, somehow, imagine Isabella at school. She was totally unlike the ordinary product of an English boarding school. Still, presumably it takes all sorts to make a school.

Across the terrace came running a brown squirrel. It sat up, looking at us. It chattered a while, then darted off to run up a tree.

I felt suddenly as though a kaleidoscopic universe had shifted, setting into a different pattern. What I saw now was the pattern of a sentient world where existence was everything, thought and speculation nothing. Here were morning and evening, day and night, food and drink, cold and heat—here movement, purpose, consciousness that did not yet know it *was* consciousness. This was the squirrel's world, the world of green grass pushing steadily upward, of trees, living and breathing. Here in this world, Isabella had her place. And strangely enough I, the broken wreck of a man, could find my place also. . . .

For the first time since my accident I ceased to rebel . . . the bitterness, the frustration, the morbid self-consciousness left me. I was no longer Hugh Norreys, twisted away from his path of active and purposeful manhood. I was Hugh Norreys, the cripple, conscious of sunshine, of a stirring breathing world, of my own rhythmic breathing, of the fact that this was a day in eternity going on its way towards sleep. . . .

The feeling did not last. But for a moment or two I had known a world in which I belonged. I suspected that it was the world in which Isabella always lived.

CHAPTER SEVEN

It must, I think, have been a day or two after that that a child fell into St. Loo harbor. Some children had been playing in a group on the edge of the quay, and one of them, screaming and running away in the course of the game, tripped and fell headlong over the edge down twenty feet into the water below. It was half-tide and there was about twelve feet of water in the harbor.

Major Gabriel who happened to be walking along the quay at the time, did not hesitate. He plunged straight in after the child. About twenty-five people crowded to the edge. By the steps on the far side a fisherman pushed off a boat and began rowing towards them. But before he could get to them, another man had dived in to the rescue having grasped the fact that Major Gabriel could not swim.

The incident ended happily. Gabriel and the child were rescued—the child unconscious but quickly brought round by artificial respiration. The child's mother, in acute hysteria, more or less fell upon Gabriel's neck, sobbing out thanks and blessings. Gabriel pooh-poohed it all, patted her on the shoulder and hurried off to the St. Loo Arms for dry clothes and alcoholic refreshment.

Later in the day, Carslake brought him along to tea.

"Pluckiest thing I ever saw in my life," he said to Teresa. "Not a moment's hesitation. Might easily have been drowned—remarkable that he *wasn't* drowned."

But Gabriel himself was properly modest and depreciatory.

"Just a damn silly thing to do," he said. "Much more to the point if I'd dashed for help or got a boat out. Trouble is, one doesn't stop to think."

Teresa said, "One of these days you'll do just one dashing thing too many."

She said it rather drily. Gabriel shot her a quick look.

After she had gone out with the tea things and Carslake had excused himself on the plea of work, Gabriel said meditatively:

"She's sharp, isn't she?"

"Who is?"

"Mrs. Norreys. She knows what's what. You can't really put much over on her." He added that he'd have to be careful.

Then he inquired, "Did I sound all right?"

I asked him what on earth he meant.

"My attitude. It was the right one, wasn't it? I mean —pooh-pooh the whole thing. Make out that I'd just been rather an ass?"

He smiled engagingly, and added:

"You don't mind my asking you, do you? It's awfully hard for me to know if I'm getting my effects right."

"Do you have to calculate effects? Can't you just be natural?"

He said meditatively that that would hardly do.

"I can't very well come in here and rub my hands with satisfaction and say, 'What a godsend!' can I?"

"Is that what you really think it was? A godsend?"

"My dear fellow, I've been going around all keyed up looking for something in that line to turn up. You know, runaway horses, burning buildings, snatching a child from under the wheels of a car. Children are the best for sob stuff purposes. You'd think with all the fuss in the papers about death on the roads, that an opportunity would come soon enough. But it hasn't—either bad luck, or else the children of St. Loo are just damnably cautious little brutes."

"You didn't give that child a shilling to throw itself into the harbor, did you?" I inquired.

He took my remark quite seriously and replied that the whole thing had happened quite naturally.

"Anyway, I wouldn't risk doing a thing like that. The kid would probably tell its mother, and then where should I be?"

I burst out laughing.

"But look here," I said. "Is it really true that you can't swim?"

"I can keep myself afloat for about three strokes."

"But then weren't you taking a frightful risk? You might easily have been drowned."

"I might have been, I suppose . . . but look here, Norreys, you can't have it both ways. You can't go in for heroism unless you're prepared to be more or less heroic. Anyway, there were lots of people about. None of them wanted to get wet, of course, but somebody would be bound to do something about it. They'd do it for the kid if they wouldn't do it for me. And there were boats. The fellow who jumped in after me held up the kid and the man with the boat arrived before I finally went under. In any case artificial respiration usually brings you back even if you have more or less drowned."

His own particular engaging grin spread across his face.

"It's all so damned silly, isn't it?" he said. "People, I mean, are such damned fools. I shall get far more kudos for going in after that kid when I couldn't swim, than if I had dived in and saved her in the approved life-saving scientific way. Lots of people are going about now saying how damned plucky it was. If they'd any sense they'd say it was just plain damned stupid—which it was. The fellow who really did the trick—the fellow who went in after me and saved us both—he won't get half as much kudos. He's a first class swimmer. He's ruined a good suit, poor devil, and my being floundering there as well as the child just made things more difficult for him. But nobody will look at it that way—unless, perhaps, it's people like your sister-in-law, but there aren't many of them.

"Just as well that there aren't," he added. "The last thing you want in an election is a lot of people who think things out and really use their heads."

"Didn't you feel a qualm or two before you jumped? An uneasy feeling in the pit of the stomach?"

"I hadn't time for that. I was just so blissfully exultant that the thing was being handed to me on a platter."

"I'm not sure that I see why you think this—this sort of spectacular business is necessary."

His face changed. It became grim and determined.

"Don't you realize that I've only got the one asset? I've no looks to speak of. I'm not a first class speaker. I've no background—no influence. I've no money. I was born with one talent—" he laid a hand on my knee—"physical courage. Do you think, if I hadn't been a V.C. that I'd ever have been put up as Conservative candidate here?"

"But, my dear fellow, isn't a V.C. enough for you?"

"You don't understand psychology, Norreys. One silly stunt like this morning, has far more effect than a V.C. gained in Southern Italy. Italy's a long way off. They didn't see me win that V.C.—and unfortunately I can't tell them about it. I could make them see it all right if I did tell them. . . . I'd take them along with me and by the time I'd finished, they'd have won that V.C. too! But the conventions of this country don't allow me to do that. No, I've got to look modest and mutter that it was nothing— any chap could have done it. Which is nonsense—very few chaps could have done what I did. Half a dozen in the regiment could have—not more. You want judgment, you know, and calculation and the coolness not to be flurried, and you've got in a way to enjoy what you're doing."

He was silent for a moment or two. Then he said, "I meant to get a V.C. when I joined up."

"My dear Gabriel!"

He turned his ugly intent little face towards me, with the shining eyes.

"You're right—you can't say definitely you'll get a thing like that. You've got to have luck. But I meant to try for it. I saw then that it was my big chance. Bravery's about the last thing you need in everyday life—it's hardly ever called for, and it's long odds against its getting you anywhere if it does. But war's different—war's where bravery comes into its own. I'm not putting on any frills about it—it's all a matter of nerves or glands or something. It just boils down to the fact that you just don't happen to be afraid of dying. You can see what an enormous advantage that gives you over the other man in a war.

"Of course I couldn't be certain that my chance would ever come. . . . You can go on being quietly brave all through a war and come out of it without a single medal. Or you can be reckless at the wrong moment and get blown to bits with nobody thanking you for it."

"Most V.C.s are posthumous," I murmured.

"Oh I know. I wonder I'm not one of them. When I think how those bullets went singing round my head, I simply can't imagine why I'm here today. Four of them got me—and not one in a vulnerable spot. Odd, wasn't it? I shall never forget the pain of dragging myself along with my broken leg. That, and the loss of blood from my shoulder . . . and then old Spider James to haul along—he never stopped cursing—and the weight of him—"

Gabriel meditated for a minute, then he sighed and said:

"Oh well, happy days," and went and got himself a drink.

"I owe you a debt of gratitude," I said, "for debunking the popular belief that all brave men are modest."

"It's a damned shame," said Gabriel. "If you're a city magnate and bring off a smart deal, you can boast about it and everyone thinks more of you. And you can admit you've painted a pretty good picture. As for golf, if you do a round under bogey, everyone hears the good news. But this war hero stuff—" he shook his head. "You've got to get another fellow to blow the trumpet for you. Carslake's not really any good at that kind of thing. He's been bitten by the Tory bug of understatement. All they do is attack the other fellow instead of blowing their own trumpet." He meditated again. "I've asked my Brigadier to come down here and speak next week. He might put it about in a quiet kind of way what a really remarkable fellow I am—but of course I can't ask him to. Awkward!"

"What with that and today's little incident, you ought not to do too badly," I said.

"Don't underestimate today's incident," said Gabriel. "You'll see. It will set everyone talking about my V.C. again. Bless that kid. I'll go around and give her a doll or something tomorrow. That will be good publicity too."

"Just tell me," I said, "a matter of curiosity. If there had been nobody there to see what happened—nobody at all, would you still have gone in after her?"

"What would have been the use if there had been nobody to see? We'd both have been drowned and nobody would have known about it until the tide washed us up somewhere."

"Then you would have walked home and let her drown?"

"No, of course not. What do you take me for? I'm a humane man. I'd have sprinted like mad round to the steps, got a boat and rowed like fury to where she'd gone in. With any luck I'd have fished her out and she'd have come round all right. I'd have done what I thought gave *her* the best chance. I like kids." He added, "Do you think the Board of Trade will give me some extra coupons for those clothes I ruined? Don't think I can ever wear that suit again. It's shrunk to nothing. These Government departments are so mean."

On this practical note he departed.

I speculated a good deal about John Gabriel. I could not decide whether I liked the man or not. His blatant opportunism rather disgusted me—his frankness was attractive. As to the accuracy of his judgment, I soon had ample confirmation of the correct way he had gauged public opinion.

Lady Tressilian was the first person to give me her views. She had brought me some books.

"You know," she said breathlessly, "I always did feel there was something really nice about Major Gabriel. This proves it, don't you think so?"

I said, "In what way?"

"Not counting the cost. Just jumping into the water although he couldn't swim."

"It wasn't much good, was it? I mean, he could never have rescued the child without help."

"No, but he didn't stop to think about that. What I admire is the brave impulse, the absence of all calculation."

I could have told her that there was plenty of calculation. She went on, her round pudding face flushing like a girl's:

"I do so admire a *really* brave man . . ."

One up to John Gabriel, I thought.

Mrs. Carslake, a feline and gushing woman whom I did not like, was positively maudlin.

"The pluckiest thing I've ever heard of. I'd been told, you know, that Major Gabriel's gallantry during the war was simply *incredible*. He absolutely didn't know what fear was. All his men *worshipped* him. For sheer heroism his record is just *too* wonderful. His C.O. is coming down here on Thursday. I shall pump him shamelessly. Of course Major Gabriel would be angry if he knew what I meant to do—he's so modest, isn't he?"

"That is the impression he manages to give, certainly," I said.

She did not notice any ambiguity in my wording.

"But I do think that these wonderful wonderful boys of ours ought not to hide their light under a bushel. It ought to be *known* all the splendid things they've done. Men are so *inarticulate*. I think it's the duty of women to spread these things abroad. Our present Member, Wilbraham, you know, he's never been out of an office all through the war."

Well, I supposed John Gabriel would say that she had the right ideas, but I did not like Mrs. Carslake. She gushed, and even as she gushed, her small dark eyes were mean and calculating.

"It's a pity, isn't it," she said, "that Mr. Norreys is a Communist."

"Every family," I said, "has its black sheep."

"They have such dreadful ideas—attack property."

"They attack other things," I said. "The Resistance movement in France is largely Communist."

That was rather a poser for Mrs. Carslake—and she retired.

Mrs. Bigham Charteris, calling in for some circulars to distribute had also her views on the harbor incident.

"Must be good blood in him somewhere," she said.

"You think so?"

"Sure to be."

"His father was a plumber," I said.

Mrs. Bigham Charteris took that in her stride.

"I imagined something of the kind. But there's good blood somewhere—far back perhaps."

She went on.

"We must have him over at the Castle a bit more. I'll talk to Adelaide. She has an unfortunate manner sometimes—it makes people ill at ease. I never felt we saw Major Gabriel at his best there. Personally, I get on with him very well."

"He seems popular in the place generally."

"Yes, he's doing very well. A good choice. The Party needs new blood—needs it badly."

She paused and said, "He might be, you know, another Disraeli."

"You think he'll go far."

"I think he might get to the top. He's got the vitality."

Lady St. Loo's comment on the affair was brought to me by Teresa who had been over to the Castle.

"Hm!" she had said. "Did it with an eye on the gallery, of course—"

I could understand why Gabriel usually referred to Lady St. Loo as an old bitch.

CHAPTER EIGHT

The weather remained fine. I spent much of my time pushed out onto the sunny terrace. There were rose beds along it and a very old yew tree at one end of it. From there I could look across to the sea and the battlements of St. Loo Castle, and I could see Isabella walking across the fields from the Castle to Polnorth House.

She had formed the habit of walking over most days. Sometimes she had the dogs with her, sometimes she was alone. When she arrived she would smile, say good morning to me, and sit on the big carved stone seat near my invalid chair.

It was an odd friendship, but friendship was what it was. It was not kindness to an invalid, not pity, not sympathy that brought Isabella to me. It was something that was, from my point of view, much better. It was liking. Because she liked me Isabella came and sat in the garden beside me. She did it as naturally and as deliberately as an animal might have done.

When we talked, we talked mostly about the things we could see; the shape of a cloud, the light on the sea, the behavior of a bird . . .

It was a bird that showed me another facet of Isabella's nature. The bird was a dead bird; it had dashed its head against the glass of the drawing room window and lay there under the window on the terrace, its legs sticking pathetically, stiffly up in the air, its soft bright eyes closed.

Isabella saw it first and the shock and horror in her voice gave me quite a start.

"Look," she said. "It's a bird—dead."

It was the note of panic in her voice that made me look so searchingly at her. She was looking like a frightened horse, her lips drawn back and quivering.

"Pick it up," I said.

She shook her head vehemently.

"I can't touch it."

"Do you dislike touching birds?" I asked. Some people did, I knew.

"I can't touch anything *dead*."

I stared at her.

She said, "I'm afraid of death—horribly afraid. I can't bear *anything* to be dead. I suppose it reminds me that I —that I shall be dead myself one day."

"We shall all be dead someday," I said.

(I was thinking of what lay at that moment conveniently close to my hand.)

"And don't you mind? Don't you mind terribly? To think it's there ahead of you—coming nearer all the time. And one day," her long beautiful hands, so seldom dramatic, struck her breast, *"it will come*. The end of living."

"What an odd girl you are, Isabella," I said. "I never knew you felt like this."

She said bitterly, "It's lucky, isn't it, that I'm a girl and not a boy. In the war I should have had to be a soldier —and I'd have disgraced us—run away or something. Yes," she spoke quietly again, almost meditatively, "it's terrible to be a coward. . . ."

I laughed a little uncertainly.

"I don't suppose you would have been a coward when the time came. Most people are—well—really it's afraid of being afraid."

"Were you afraid?"

"Good Lord, yes!"

"But when it came it was—all right?"

I cast my mind back to a particular moment—the strain of waiting in darkness—waiting for the order to move forward . . . the sick feeling in the pit of the stomach. . . .

I was truthful.

"No," I said. "I wouldn't describe it as all right. But I found that I could more or less take it. That is to say, I could take it as well as anybody else. You see, after a bit, you get into the way of feeling that it's never you who are going to stop the bullet—it may be the other fellow, but not you."

"Do you think Major Gabriel felt like that, too?"

I paid Gabriel his tribute.

"I rather fancy," I said, "that Gabriel is one of the rare and lucky people who simply don't know what fear is."

"Yes," she said. "I thought that, too."

There was a queer expression on her face.

I asked her if she had always been afraid of death. If she had had some shock that had given her a special terror.

She shook her head.

"I don't think so. Of course, my father was killed before I was born. I don't know if that—"

"Yes," I said, "I think that's very likely. I think that would account for it."

Isabella was frowning. Her mind was on the past.

"My canary died when I was about five. It was quite well the night before—and in the morning it was lying in the cage—with its feet sticking up stiff—like that bird just now. I took it in my hand," she shivered. "It was cold . . ." She struggled with words. "It—it wasn't *real* any more . . . it was just a *thing* . . . it didn't see . . . or hear . . . or feel . . . it—it wasn't *there!*"

And suddenly, almost pathetically, she asked of me:

"Don't you think it's awful that we have to die?"

I don't know what I ought to have said. Instead of a considered reply I blurted out the truth—my own particular truth.

"Sometimes—it's the only thing a man has got to look forward to."

She looked at me with blank uncomprehending eyes.

"I don't know what you mean . . ."

"Don't you?" I said bitterly. "Use your eyes, Isabella. What do you think life is like, washed, dressed, got up in the morning like a baby, hauled about like a sack of coals—an inanimate useless broken hulk, lying here in the sun with nothing to do and nothing to look forward to, and nothing to hope for. . . . If I was a broken chair or table they'd throw me on the junk heap—but because I'm a man they put civilized garments on me, and throw a rug over the worst of the wreckage and lay me out here in the sun!"

Her eyes grew wide, wide with puzzlement, with questioning. For the first time, or so it seemed to me, they looked not beyond me but at me. They focused on me. And even then they saw and understood nothing—nothing but bare physical facts.

She said, "But at any rate you *are* in the sun . . . You *are* alive. You might easily have been killed . . ."

"Very easily. Don't you understand that I wish to God I had been killed?"

No, she didn't understand. To her, it was a foreign language I was speaking. She said, almost timidly:

"Are you—in a lot of pain always? Is it *that?*"

"I have a good deal of pain from time to time, but no, Isabella, it's not that. Can't you understand that I've nothing to live *for?*"

"But—I know I'm stupid—does one have to have anything to live for? I mean why? Can't one just live?"

I caught my breath before the simplicity of that.

And then, as I turned, or tried to turn on my couch, an awkward gesture on my part jerked the little bottle labelled Aspirin out of the place I kept it onto the grass and in falling the cap fell off and the little tablets inside scattered far and wide all over the grass.

I almost screamed. I heard my voice, hysterical, unnatural, calling out:

"Don't let them be lost . . . oh, pick them up . . . find them . . . don't let them go!"

Isabella bent, deftly picking up the tablets. Turning my head, I saw Teresa coming through the window. It was with almost a sob in my voice that I cried out under my breath:

"Teresa's coming . . ."

And then, to my astonishment, Isabella did something of which I would never have suspected her capable.

With a single rapid but unflurried gesture she loosened the colored scarf she was wearing round the neck of her summer frock, and let it float down on the grass covering the sprawled tablets. . . . And at the same time she said in a quiet conversational voice:

"—you see, everything may be quite different when Rupert comes home—"

You would have sworn that we were in the middle of a conversation.

Teresa came to us and asked:

"What about a drink, you two?"

I suggested something rather elaborate. As Teresa was turning back to the house, she half bent as though to pick up the scarf. Isabella said in her unhurried voice:

"Do leave it, Mrs. Norreys—the colors look nice against the grass."

Teresa smiled and went back through the window.

I was left staring at Isabella.

"My dear girl," I said, "why did you do that?"

She looked at me shyly.

"I thought," she said, "that you didn't want her to see them. . . ."

"You thought right," I said grimly.

In the early days of my convalescence I had formed a plan. I foresaw only too plainly my helpless state, my complete dependence on others. I wanted a means of exit ready to my hand.

So long as they injected morphia, I could no nothing. But there came a time when morphia was replaced by sleeping draughts or tablets. That was my opportunity. At first I cursed, for I was given chloral in draught form. But later, when I was with Robert and Teresa, and medical attendance was less frequent, the doctor prescribed sleeping tablets—seconal, I think, or it may have been amytal. In any case there was an arrangement by which I was to try and do without the tablets, but a couple were left handy to take if sleep did not come. Little by little I accumulated my store. I continued to complain of sleeplessness, and fresh tablets were prescribed. I endured long nights of pain wide-eyed, fortified by the knowledge that my gate of departure was opening wider. For some time now I had had enough and more than enough to do the trick.

And with the accomplishment of my project, the urgent need for it retreated. I was content to wait a little while longer. But I did not mean to wait forever.

For an agonized few minutes, I had seen my plan jeopardized, retarded, perhaps ruined altogether. From that disaster Isabella's quick wits had saved me. She was picking up the tablets now and replacing them in the bottle. Presently she gave it to me.

I put the bottle back in its place and breathed a deep sigh.

"Thank you, Isabella," I said with feeling.

She showed no curiosity, no anxiety. She had been astute enough to realize my agitation and to come to my rescue. I apologized mentally for having once thought her a moron. She was no fool.

What did she think? She must have realized that those tablets were something other than aspirin.

I looked at her. There was no clue at all to what she thought. I found her very difficult to understand . . .

And then a sudden curiosity stirred in me.

She had mentioned a name . . .

"Who is Rupert?" I said.

"Rupert is my cousin."

"You mean Lord St. Loo?"

"Yes. He may be coming here soon. He's been in Burma during most of the war." She paused and said, "He may come here to live . . . the Castle is his, you know. We only rent it."

"I just wondered," I said, "why—well, why you suddenly mentioned him."

"I just wanted to say something quickly to make it seem as though we were talking." Then she meditated a minute. "I suppose—I spoke of Rupert—because I am always thinking of him. . . ."

CHAPTER NINE

Up to now Lord St. Loo had been a name, an abstraction—the absent owner of St. Loo Castle. Now he came into the round—a living entity. I began to wonder about him.

Lady Tressilian came over in the afternoon to bring me what she described as "a book I thought might interest you." It was not, I saw at a glance, the kind of book that would interest me. It was the kind of smartly written pep talk that wants you to believe that you can make the world brighter and better by lying on your back and thinking beautiful thoughts. Lady Tressilian, her thwarted maternal instincts asserting themselves, was always bringing me something. Her favorite idea was that I should become an author. She had brought me the literature of at least three correspondence courses on "How to make a living by writing in twenty-four lessons" or something of that kind. She was one of those nice kind women who cannot, by any possible chance, leave anyone who is suffering to suffer alone.

I could not dislike her, but I could, and did, try to dodge her ministrations. Sometimes Teresa helped, but sometimes she didn't. Sometimes she looked at me, smiled, and deliberately left me to my fate. When I swore at her afterwards she said that a counter irritant was a good thing occasionally.

On this particular afternoon Teresa was out on political canvassing, so I had no chance of escape.

When Lady Tressilian had sighed and asked me how I was and told me how much better I was looking and I had thanked her for the book and said it looked very interesting, we dropped into local chat. At the moment all our local chat was political. She told me how the meetings had gone and how well Gabriel had tackled some hecklers. She went on to talk of what the country really wanted and how terrible it would be if everything was nationalized, and how unscrupulous the other side were, and exactly what the farmers felt about the Milk Marketing Board. The conversation was practically identical with one we had had three days ago.

It was then, after a slight pause, that Lady Tressilian sighed and said how wonderful it would be if Rupert came soon.

"Is there a chance of it?" I asked.

"Yes. He was wounded—out in Burma, you know. It is so wicked the newspapers hardly mention the Fourteenth Army. He has been in hospital for some time, and he is due for a long spell of leave. There are a lot of things for him to settle here. We have all done the best we can, but conditions are changing the whole time."

I gathered that with taxation and other difficulties, Lord St. Loo would probably soon have to sell some of his land.

"The part by the sea is good building land, but one hates

to have more of those dreadful little houses springing up."

I agreed that the builders who had developed the East Cliff had not been overburdened with artistic sensibility.

She said, "My brother-in-law, the seventh Lord St. Loo, gave that land to the town. He wanted it to be saved for the people, but he did not think of attaching specific safeguards, and consequently the Council sold it all, bit by bit, for building. It was very dishonest, for it was *not* what my brother-in-law meant."

I asked if Lord St. Loo was thinking of coming here to live.

"I don't know. He has not said anything definite." She sighed. "I hope so—I do very much hope so."

She added, "We have not seen him since he was sixteen—he used to come here for his holidays when he was at Eton. His mother was a New Zealander—a very charming girl—when she was left a widow she went back to her own people and took the child with her. One cannot blame her, and yet I always regret that the boy was not brought up on what was to be his own estate from the beginning. He is bound, I feel, when he comes here, to be out of touch. But then, of course, everything is changing . . ."

Her nice round face looked distressed.

"We have done our best. Death duties were heavy. Isabella's father was killed in the last war. The place had got to be let. By clubbing together Addie and I and Maud could manage to rent it—and it seemed so much better than letting it to strangers. It has always been Isabella's home."

Her face softened as she bent towards me confidentially.

"I daresay I am a very sentimental old woman, but I have so hoped that Isabella and Rupert—it would be, I mean, the *ideal* solution . . ."

I did not speak and she went on:

"Such a handsome boy—so charming and affectionate to us all—and he always seemed to have a special fondness for Isabella. She was only eleven then. She used to follow him about everywhere. She was quite devoted to him. Addie and I used to look at them and say to each other, 'If only—' Maud, of course, kept saying that they were first cousins and it wouldn't do. But then Maud is always thinking of things from the pedigree point of view. Lots of first cousins do marry and it turns out quite all right. It's not as though we were an R.C. family and had to get a dispensation."

Again she paused. This time her face had that absorbed, intensely feminine expression that women put on when they are matchmaking.

"He has always remembered her birthday every year. He writes to Asprey's. I think, don't you, that that is rather touching? Isabella is such a dear girl—and she loves St. Loo so much." She looked out towards the battlements of the castle. "If they could settle down there together . . ." I saw tears gathering in her eyes. . . .

("This place becomes more like a fairy story than ever," I said to Teresa that evening. "A fairy Prince may arrive any minute to marry the Princess. Where *are* we living? In a story from Grimms?")

"Tell me about your cousin Rupert," I said to Isabella when she was sitting on the stone seat the next day.

"I don't think there is anything to tell."

"You think about him all the time, you said. Is that really true?"

She considered for a moment or two.

"No, I don't think about him. I meant—he is there in my mind. I think—that one day I shall marry Rupert."

She turned towards me as though my silence disquieted her.

"Does that seem to you an absurd thing to say? I haven't seen Rupert since I was eleven and he was sixteen. He said then he would come back and marry me someday. I've always believed it . . . I still believe it."

"And Lord and Lady St. Loo were married and lived happy ever afterwards in St. Loo Castle by the sea," I said.

"You think it won't happen?" Isabella asked.

She looked at me as though my opinion on the point might be final.

I drew a deep breath.

"I'm inclined to think it will happen. It's that kind of fairy story."

We were recalled bluntly from fairy stories to reality by Mrs. Bigham Charteris who made an abrupt appearance on the terrace.

She had a bulging parcel with her which she flapped down beside her, requesting me brusquely to give it to Captain Carslake.

"I think he's in his office," I began, but she interrupted:

"I know—but I don't want to go in there. I'm not in the mood for that woman."

Personally I was never in the mood for Mrs. Carslake, but I saw that there was something more than that behind Mrs. Bigham Charteris' almost violently brusque manner.

Isabella saw it too. She asked:

"Is anything the matter, Aunt Maud?"

Mrs. Bigham Charteris, her face rigid, jerked out:

"Lucinda's been run over."

Lucinda was Mrs. Bigham Charteris' brown spaniel whom she adored passionately.

She went on, speaking still more jerkily, and fixing me with a glacial eye to prevent me expressing sympathy:

"Down by the quay—some of those bloody tourists—driving much too fast—didn't even stop— Come on, Isabella—we must get home—"

I didn't offer tea or sympathy.

Isabella asked, "Where is Lucy?"

"Took her into Burt's. Major Gabriel helped me. He was very kind, very kind indeed."

Gabriel had come upon the scene when Lucinda was lying whimpering in the road and Mrs. Bigham Charteris was kneeling by her. He had knelt down also and had felt the dog's body all over with skillful sensitive fingers.

He said:

"There's a loss of power in the hind legs—it might be internal injury. We ought to get her to a vet."

"I always have Johnson from Polwithen—he's wonderful with dogs. But that's too far."

He nodded. "Who's the best vet in St. Loo?"

"James Burt. He's clever, but he's a brute. I'd never

trust him with dogs—not to send them to his place. He drinks, you know. But he's quite near here. We'd better take Lucy there. Mind—she may bite."

Gabriel said with confidence:

"She won't bite me." He spoke to her soothingly. "All right, old girl, all right." He slid his arms under her gently. The crowd of small boys, fishermen and young women with shopping bags made sympathetic noises and offered advice.

Mrs. Bigham Charteris said jerkily, "Good girl, Lucy, good girl."

To Gabriel she said, "It's very kind of you. Burt's house is just round the corner in Western Place."

It was a prim Victorian house, slate-roofed, with a worn brass plate on the gate.

The door was opened by a rather pretty woman of about twenty-eight who turned out to be Mrs. Burt.

She recognized Mrs. Bigham Charteris at once.

"Oh, Mrs. Bigham Charteris, I'm ever so sorry. My husband's out. And the assistant too."

"When will he be back?"

"I think Mr. Burt will be back any minute now. Of course, his surgery hours are nine to ten or two to three—but I'm sure he'll do all he can. What's the matter with the dog? Run over?"

"Yes, just now—by a car."

"It's wicked, isn't it?" said Milly Burt. "They go far too fast. Bring her into the surgery, will you?"

She talked on in her soft, slightly over-refined voice. Mrs. Bigham Charteris stood by Lucinda, stroking her. Her weatherbeaten face was twisted with pain. She could pay no attention to Milly Burt, who talked on, kindly, inadequately, rather at a loss.

She said presently that she would telephone to Lower Grange Farm and see if Mr. Burt was there. The telephone was in the hall. Gabriel went with her, leaving Mrs. Bigham Charteris alone with her dog and her own agony. He was a perceptive man.

Mrs. Burt dialled the number, and recognized the voice at the other end.

"Yes, Mrs. Whidden—it's Mrs. Burt speaking. Is Mr. Burt there—well, yes, I would if you don't mind—yes—" There was a pause, and then Gabriel, watching her, saw her flush and wince. Her voice changed—it became apologetic—timid.

"I'm sorry, Jim. No, of course—" Gabriel could hear the sound of Burt's voice at the other end, though not what he said—a domineering, ugly voice. Milly Burt's voice became more apologetic.

"It's Mrs. Bigham Charteris—from the Castle—her dog—it's been run over. Yes, she's here now."

She flushed again and replaced the receiver, but not before Gabriel had heard the voice at the other end say angrily:

"Why couldn't you say so at once, you fool?"

There was a moment's awkwardness. Gabriel felt sorry for Mrs. Burt—a pretty gentle little thing, scared of that husband of hers. He said in his sincere friendly way:

"It's awfully good of you to take so much trouble and to be so sympathetic, Mrs. Burt." And he smiled at her.

"Oh, that's quite all right, Major Gabriel. It *is* Major Gabriel, isn't it?" She was just a little excited by his appearance in her house. "I came to your meeting in the Institute the other night."

"That was very nice of you, Mrs. Burt."

"And I do hope you get in—but I'm sure you will. Everybody's dreadfully tired of Mr. Wilbraham, I'm sure. He doesn't really belong here, you know. He's not a Cornishman."

"No more am I for that matter."

"Oh, *you*—"

She looked at him with eyes that were rather like Lucinda's brown eyes, capable of hero worship. Her hair was brown, too, pretty chestnut hair. Her lips parted, she was looking at John Gabriel, seeing him against a background of no particular place—just as a figure against a war landscape. Desert, heat, shots, blood, staggering over open country. . . . A film landscape like the picture she'd seen last week.

And he was no natural—so kind—so *ordinary!*

Gabriel exerted himself to talk to her. He particularly didn't want her to go back into the surgery and worry that poor old bean who wanted to be alone with her dog. Especially as he was fairly sure the dog was for it. Pity, a lovely bitch and not more than three or four years old. This was a nice little woman, but she would want to show her sympathy by talking. She'd go on and on, exclaiming about motors and the number of dogs killed each year, and what a lovely dog Lucinda was, and wouldn't Mrs. Charteris like a cup of tea?

So John Gabriel talked to Milly Burt, and made her laugh, so that she showed her pretty teeth and a nice dimple that she had at one corner of her mouth. She was looking quite lively and animated when the door suddenly opened and a thickset man in riding breeches stumped in.

Gabriel was startled by the way Burt's wife flinched and shrank.

"Oh, Jim—here you are," she exclaimed nervously. "This is Major Gabriel."

James Burt nodded curtly and his wife went on:

"Mrs. Charteris is in the surgery with the dog—"

Burt interrupted: "Why didn't you take the dog in there and keep her out? You never have the least sense."

"Shall I ask her—"

"I'll see to it."

He shouldered his way past her and went down the stairs into the surgery.

Milly Burt blinked hasty tears out of her eyes.

She asked Major Gabriel if he would like a cup of tea.

Because he was sorry for Mrs. Burt and because he thought her husband was an unmannerly brute, he said he would.

And that was the beginning of that.

CHAPTER TEN

It was, I think, the following day—or possibly the day after —that Teresa brought Mrs. Burt into my sitting room.

She said, "This is my brother-in-law, Hugh. Hugh, this is Mrs. Burt who has kindly offered to help us."

"Us" was not personal but denoted the Conservative Party.

I looked at Teresa. She did not bat an eyelash. Mrs. Burt was already yearning over me with soft brown eyes full of womanly sympathy. If I had occasionally indulged in the luxury of pitying myself, moments such as these were wholesome correctives. Against the eager sympathy in Mrs. Burt's eyes I had no defence. Teresa basely left the room.

Mrs. Burt sat down beside me and prepared to be chatty. When I had recovered from my self-consciousness and raw misery, I was forced to admit that she was a nice woman.

"I do feel," she was saying, "that we must all do what we can for the election. I'm afraid I can't do much. I'm not clever. I couldn't go and talk to people, but as I said to Mrs. Norreys if there is any clerical work to be done, or leaflets to be delivered, I could do that. I thought Major Gabriel spoke so splendidly at the Institute about the part women can play. It made me feel I'd been terribly slack up to now. He's such a wonderful speaker, don't you think? Oh, I forgot—I suppose you—?"

Her distress was rather touching. She looked at me in a dismayed fashion. I came to her rescue quickly.

"I heard his opening speech at the Drill Hall. He certainly gets his effects."

She suspected no irony. She said with a rush of feeling: "I think he's splendid."

"That's exactly what we—er—want everyone to think."

"So they ought," said Milly Burt. "I mean—it will make all the difference to have a man like that standing for St. Loo. A real man. A man who's really been in the Army and fought. Mr. Wilbraham is all right, of course, but I always think these socialists are so cranky—and after all, he's only a schoolmaster or something of that sort—and very weedy looking and such an affected voice. One doesn't feel he's really *done* things."

I listened to the voice of the electorate with some interest, and observed that John Gabriel had certainly done things.

She flushed with enthusiasm.

"I've heard he's one of the bravest men in the whole Army. They say he could have won the V.C. over and over again."

Gabriel had evidently succeeded in getting the right kind of publicity across. That is, unless it was just personal enthusiasm on the part of Mrs. Burt. She was looking very pretty with her cheeks slightly flushed and her brown eyes alight with hero worship.

"He came in with Mrs. Bigham Charteris," she explained. "The day her dog was run over. It was nice of him, wasn't it? He was ever so concerned about it."

"Possibly he's fond of dogs," I said.

That was a little too ordinary for Milly Burt.

"No," she said. "I think it's because he is so kind—so wonderfully kind. And he talked so naturally and so pleasantly."

She paused and went on, "I felt quite ashamed. I mean, ashamed that I hadn't been doing more to help the cause. Of course, I always vote Conservative, but just voting isn't nearly enough, is it?"

"That," I said, "is a matter of opinion."

"So I really felt I must do *something*—and I came along to ask Captain Carslake what I can do. I've really got a lot of time on my hands, you see. Mr. Burt is so busy— out all day except just for surgery—and I haven't any children."

A different expression showed in her brown eyes for a moment—I felt sorry for her. She was the kind of woman who ought to have had children. She would have made a very good mother.

The thwarted maternity was still in her face as she abandoned her memories of John Gabriel and concentrated on me instead.

"You were wounded at Alamein, weren't you?" she said.

"No," I said furiously, "in the Harrow Road."

"Oh." She was taken aback. "But Major Gabriel told me—"

"Gabriel would," I said. "You mustn't believe a word he says."

She smiled doubtfully. She admitted a joke that she couldn't quite see.

"You look wonderfully fit," she said encouragingly.

"My dear Mrs. Burt, I neither look fit nor feel it."

She said, very nicely, "I'm really dreadfully sorry, Captain Norreys."

Before I could attempt murder, the door opened and Carslake and Gabriel came in.

Gabriel did his stuff very well. His face lighted up and he came across to her.

"Hullo, Mrs. Burt. This *is* nice of you! It really is nice."

She looked happy and shy.

"Oh, really, Major Gabriel—I don't suppose I shall be any use. But I do want to do *something* to help."

"You are going to help. We're going to make you *work*." He had her hand still in his and was smiling all over his ugly face. I could feel the charm and the magnetism of the man—and if I felt it, the woman felt it far more. She laughed and flushed.

"I'll do my best. It's important, isn't it, that we should show that the country is loyal to Mr. Churchill?"

It was far more important, I could have told her, that we should be loyal to John Gabriel and return him with a good majority.

"That's the spirit," said Gabriel heartily. "It's the women who have the real power in elections nowadays. If only they'll use it."

"Oh, I know." She was grave. "We don't *care* enough."

"Oh well," said Gabriel. "After all, one candidate isn't much better than another perhaps."

"Oh, Major Gabriel," she was shocked. "Of course, there is all the difference in the world."

"Yes, indeed, Mrs. Burt," said Carslake. "I can tell you Major Gabriel is going to make them sit up at Westminster."

I wanted to say "Oh yeah?" but restrained myself. Carslake took her off to give her some leaflets or some typing or something and Gabriel said as the door closed behind them:

"Nice little woman, that."

"You certainly have her eating out of your hand."

He frowned at me.

"Come off it, Norreys. I like Mrs. Burt. And I'm sorry for her. If you ask me, she hasn't got too easy a life."

"Possibly not. She doesn't look very happy."

"Burt's a callous devil. Drinks a lot. I should fancy he could be brutal. I noticed yesterday that she had a couple of nasty bruises on her arm. I bet he knocks her about. Things like that make me see red."

I was a little surprised. Gabriel noticed my surprise, and gave a vigorous nod of the head.

"I'm not putting it on. Cruelty always does rile me. . . . Have you ever thought about the kind of lives women may have to lead? And hold their tongues about?"

"There's legal redress, I suppose," I said.

"No, there isn't, Norreys—not until the last resort. Systematic bullying, steady sneering unkindness, a bit of rough stuff if he's had a drop too much—what's a woman able to do about that? What can she do but sit down under it—and suffer quietly? Women like Milly Burt have got no money of their own—where could they go if they walked out on their husbands? Relations don't like fomenting marital troubles. Women like Milly Burt are quite alone. No one will lift a finger to help them."

"Yes," I said, "that's true . . ."

I looked at him curiously.

"You're very heated?"

"Don't you think I'm capable of a little decent sympathy? I like that girl. I'm sorry for her. I wish there were anything I could do about it—but I suppose there isn't."

I stirred uneasily. Or rather, to be accurate, I tried to stir—and was rewarded by a twinge of sharp pain from my maimed body. But with the physical pain went another, more subtle pain, the pain of memory. I was sitting again in a train going from Cornwall to London and watching tears drop into a plate of soup. . . .

That was the way things started—not the way you

imagined they'd start. It was one's helplessness in face of pity that laid you open to the assaults of life, that led you —where? In my case to an invalid chair with no future before me and a past that mocked me. . . .

I said abruptly to Gabriel (and there was a connection in my mind, though to him the transition must have seemed abrupt indeed):

"How's the nice little number at the St. Loo Arms?"

He grinned.

"That's all right, my boy. I'm being very discreet. Strictly business whilst I'm in St. Loo." He sighed. "It's a pity. She's just my type. . . . But there—you can't have everything! Mustn't let down the Tory Party."

I asked if the Tory Party was so particular, and he replied that there was a very strong Puritan element in St. Loo. Fishermen, he added, tended to be religious.

"In spite of having a wife in every port?"

"That's the Navy, old boy. Don't get things mixed up."

"Well, don't *you* get mixed up—with the St. Loo Arms or with Mrs. Burt."

He flared up unexpectedly at that.

"Look here, what are you driving at? Mrs. Burt's straight—dead straight. She's a nice kid."

I looked at him curiously.

"She's all right, I tell you," he insisted. "She wouldn't stand for any funny business."

"No," I agreed. "I don't think she would. But she admires you very much, you know."

"Oh, that's the V.C. and the harbor business and various rumors that get around."

"I was going to ask you about that. Who's circulating these rumors?"

He winked.

"I'll tell you this—they're useful—very useful. Wilbraham's C.3, poor devil."

"Who starts them off—Carslake?"

Gabriel shook his head.

"Not Carslake. Too heavy-handed. I couldn't trust him. I've had to get to work myself."

I burst out laughing.

"Do you seriously mean to tell me you've got the nerve to tell people that you could have won the V.C. three times over?"

"It's not quite like that. I use women—the less brainy type. They drag details out of me—details that I'm reluctant to give them—then, when I get horribly embarrassed and beg them not to mention it to a soul, they hurry off and tell all their best friends."

"You really are shameless, Gabriel."

"I'm fighting an election. I've got my career to think of. These things count a great deal more than whether I'm sound on the subject of tariffs, or reparations, or equal pay for equally bad work. Women always go for the personal element."

"That reminds me; what the devil do you mean by telling Mrs. Burt that I was wounded at Alamein?"

Gabriel sighed.

"I suppose you disillusioned her. You shouldn't do it, old boy. Cash in on what you can while the going's good. Heroes have got a high points value just at present. They'll slump later. Cash in while you can."

"Under false pretenses?"

"Quite unnecessary to tell women the truth. I never do. They don't like it, you'll find."

"That's a little different from telling a deliberate lie."

"No need to lie. I'd done the lying for you. You'd only got to mutter, 'Nonsense . . . all a mistake . . . Gabriel should have held his tongue . . .' And then start talking about the weather—or the pilchard catch—or what's cooking in darkest Russia. And the girl goes away all big-eyed with enthusiasm. Damn it, don't you want *any* fun?"

"What fun can I have nowadays?"

"Well, I realize you can't actually go to bed with anyone—" Gabriel seldom minced his words. "But a bit of sob stuff's better than nothing. Don't you want women to make a fuss of you?"

"No."

"Funny—I should."

"I wonder."

Gabriel's face changed. He frowned. He said slowly:

"You may be right . . . I suppose when you come down to it none of us really know ourselves . . . *I* think I'm pretty well acquainted with John Gabriel. You're suggesting that I mayn't know him so well as I think I do. Meet Major John Gabriel—I don't think you know each other. . . ."

He paced swiftly up and down the room. I sensed that my words had plumbed some deep disquiet. He looked— yes, I realized it suddenly—he looked like a frightened little boy.

"You're wrong," he said. "You're dead wrong. I *do* know myself. It's the one thing I do know. Sometimes I wish I didn't . . . I know exactly what I am, and what I'm capable of. I'm careful, mind you, not to let other people catch on. I know where I've come from and I know where I'm going. I know what I want—and I mean to make sure of getting it. I've worked it all out fairly carefully—and I don't think I'm likely to slip up." He considered for a moment or two. "No, I think I'm well set. I'm going to get where I want to be!"

The ring in his voice interested me. Just for a moment I believed that John Gabriel was more than a charlatan— I saw him as a power.

"So *that's* what you want," I said. "Well—perhaps you'll get it."

"Get what?"

"Power. That's what you meant, wasn't it?"

He stared at me, then broke out laughing.

"Good Lord, no. Who do you think I am—Hitler? I don't want power—I've no ambition to lord it over my fellow creatures or the world generally. Good God, man, what do you think I'm in this racket for? Power's poppy-cock! What I want is a soft job. That's all."

I stared at him. I was disappointed. Just for a moment John Gabriel had attained titanic proportions. Now he had shrunk back again to life size. He flung himself down in a chair and thrust out his legs. I saw him suddenly as he was apart from his charm—a gross, mean little man—a greedy little man.

"And you can thank your stars," he said, "that that's

all I *do* want! Men who are greedy and self-seeking don't hurt the world—the world's got room for them. And they're the right kind of men to have governing you. Heaven help any country that has men in power with ideas! A man with an idea will grind down the common people, and starve children, and break women, without even noticing what's happening to them. He won't even *care*. But a selfish grasping bloke won't do much harm—he only wants his own little corner made comfortable, and once he's got that, he's quite agreeable to having the average man happy and contented. In fact, he prefers him happy and contented—it's less trouble. I know pretty well what most people want—it isn't much. Just to feel important and to have a chance of doing a bit better than the other man and not to be too much pushed around. You mark my words, Norreys, that's where the Labour Party will make their big mistake when they get in—"

"If they get in," I interrupted.

"They'll get in all right," said Gabriel confidently. "And I'm telling you where they'll make their mistake. They'll start pushing people round. All with the best intentions. The ones who aren't really dyed-in-the-wool Tories are cranks. And God save us from cranks! It's really remarkable the amount of suffering a really high-minded idealistic crank can inflict on a decent law-abiding country."

I argued, "It still boils down to the fact that you think you know what is best for the country?"

"Not at all. I know what's best for John Gabriel. The country's safe from my experiments because I shall be occupied thinking about myself and how to dig myself in comfortably. I don't care in the least about being Prime Minister."

"You surprise me!"

"Now don't make any mistake, Norreys, I probably *could* become Prime Minister if I wanted to. It's amazing what you can do, if you just study what people want to hear said and then say it to them! But to be Prime Minister means a lot of worry and hard work. I mean to make a name for myself, that's all—"

"And where's the money coming from? Six hundred a year doesn't go far."

"They'll have to put it up if Labour gets in. Probably make it a clear thousand. But don't make any mistake, there are plenty of ways of making money in a political career—some on the side, some straightforward. And there's marriage—"

"You've planned your marriage, too? A title?"

For some reason he flushed.

"No," he spoke with vehemence. "I'm not marrying out of my class. Oh yes, I know what my class is. I'm not a gentleman."

"Does that word mean anything nowadays?" I asked skeptically.

"The word doesn't. But the thing the word means is still there."

He stared in front of him. When he spoke his voice was reflective and far away.

"I remember going round to a big house with my father. He was doing a job on the kitchen boiler. I stayed around outside the house. A kid came and spoke to me. Nice kid, a year or two older than I was. She took me along with her into the garden—rather a super garden—fountains, you know, and terraces, and big cedar trees and green grass like velvet. Her brother was there, too. He was younger. We played games. Hide and Seek—I Spy— It was fine— we got on together like a house on fire. And then a nannie came out of the house—all starched and got up in uniform. Pam, that was the kid's name, went dancing up to her and said I must come to tea in the nursery, she wanted me to come to tea.

"I can see that stuck up nurse's face now—the primness of it, I can hear the mincing voice!

"'You can't do that, dear. He's just a common little boy.'"

Gabriel stopped. I was shocked—shocked at what cruelty, unconscious unthinking cruelty, can do. He'd been hearing that voice, seeing that face, ever since. . . . He'd been hurt—hurt to the core.

"But look here," I said, "it wasn't the children's mother.

It was—well—a very second class thing to say—apart from the cruelty—"

He turned a white somber face on me.

"You don't get the point, Norreys. I agree a gentle-woman wouldn't have said a thing like that—she'd have been more considerate—but the fact remains that it was true. I *was* a common little boy. I'm *still* a common little boy. I'll die a common little boy."

"Don't be absurd! What do these things matter?"

"They don't matter. They've left off mattering. In actual fact, it's an advantage not to be a gentleman nowadays. People sneer at those rather pathetic straight-backed old ladies and gentlemen who are well connected and haven't enough to live on. All we're snobbish about nowadays is education. Education's our fetish. But the trouble is, Norreys, that I didn't want to be a common little boy. I went home and said to my father, 'Dad, when I grow up I want to be a Lord. I want to be Lord John Gabriel.' 'And that's what you'll never be,' he said. 'You've got to be born that kind of a Lord. They can make you a Peer if you get rich enough but it's not the same thing.' And it isn't the same thing. There's something—something I can never have—oh, I don't mean the title. I mean being born sure of yourself—knowing what you're going to do or say—being rude only when you mean to be rude—and not being rude just because you feel hot and uncomfortable and want to show you're as good as anyone else. Not having to go about hot under the collar and wondering all the time what people are thinking of you, but just concerned with what *you* think of *them*. Knowing that if you're queer or shabby or eccentric it doesn't matter a damn because you are what you are . . ."

"Because, in fact, you're Lady St. Loo?" I suggested.

"Blast and damn the old bitch!" said John Gabriel.

I looked at him with considerable interest.

"You know," I said, "you're really very interesting."

"It isn't real to you, is it? You don't know what I mean. You think you do—but you don't really get near it."

"I knew," I said slowly, "that there had been something . . . that you'd had, once, some shock. . . . You were wounded as a child, hurt. In a sense you've never got over it—"

"Cut out the psychology," said Gabriel curtly. "But you see, don't you, why, when I get with a nice girl like Milly Burt, I'm happy. And that's the kind of girl I'm going to marry. She'll have to have money, of course—but money or no money she'll be of my own class. You can imagine, can't you, the Hell it would be if I married some stuck up girl with a face like a horse and spent my life trying to live up to her?"

He paused and said abruptly:

"You were in Italy. Did you ever get to Pisa?"

"I have been in Pisa—some years ago."

"I think it's Pisa I mean. . . . There's a thing there painted on the wall—Heaven and Hell and Purgatory and all the rest of it. Hell's rather jolly, little devils pushing you down with pitchforks. Heaven's up above—a row of the blessed sitting under trees with a smug expression on their faces. My God, those women! They don't know about Hell, they don't know about the damned—they don't know *anything!* They just sit there, smiling smugly—" His passion rose. "Smug, smug, self-satisfied— God, I'd like to tear them down from their trees and their state of beatitude and pitch them down into the flames! Hold them there writhing; make them feel, make them suffer! What right have they not to know what suffering is? There they sit, smiling, and nothing can ever touch them. . . . Their heads among the stars. . . . Yes, that's it, among the stars. . . ."

He got up, his voice fell, his eyes looked past me, vague searching eyes . . .

"Among the stars," he repeated.

Then he laughed.

"Sorry to have inflicted all this on you. But after all, why not? The Harrow Road may have made a pretty fair wreck of you, but you're still good for *something*—you can listen to me when I feel like talking . . . You'll find, I expect, that people will talk to you a good deal."

"I do find that."

"Do you know why? It isn't because you're such a wonderfully sympathetic listener or anything like that. It's because you're no good for anything else."

He stood, his head a little on one side, his eyes, angry eyes still, watching me. He wanted his words to hurt me, I think. But they did not hurt me. I experienced instead considerable relief in hearing put into spoken words the things that I had been thinking inside my head. . . .

"Why the Hell you don't get out of it all I can't think," he said, "or haven't you got the means?"

"I've got the means all right," I said, and my hand closed round my bottle of tablets.

"I see," he said. "You've got more guts than I thought. . . ."

CHAPTER ELEVEN

Mrs. Carslake spent some time talking to me next morning. I did not like Mrs. Carslake. She was a thin dark woman with an acid tongue. I don't think that all the time I was at Polnorth House I ever heard her say a nice thing about anyone. Sometimes, for sheer amusement, I used to mention name after name and wait for the first sweetness of her comments to go sour.

She was talking now of Milly Burt.

"She's a nice little thing," she said. "And so anxious to help. She's rather stupid, of course, and not very well educated politically. Women of that class are very apathetic politically."

It was my own impression that Milly Burt's class was also Mrs. Carslake's class. To annoy her, I said:

"Just like Teresa, in fact."

Mrs. Carslake looked shocked.

"Oh, but Mrs. Norreys is very clever—" then came the usual touch of venom—"far too clever for *me* sometimes. I get the impression often that she quite despises us all. Intellectual women are often very wrapped up in themselves, don't you think so? Of course, I wouldn't exactly call Mrs. Norreys selfish—"

Then she reverted to Milly Burt.

"It's a good thing for Mrs. Burt to have something to do," she said. "I'm afraid, you know, she has a very unhappy home life."

"I'm sorry to hear it."

"That man Burt is going right down the hill. He comes reeling out of the St. Loo Arms at closing time. Really, I wonder they serve him. And I believe he's quite violent sometimes—or so the neighbors say. She's frightened to death of him, you know."

Her nose quivered at the tip—it was, I decided, a quiver indicating pleasurable sensations.

"Why doesn't she leave him?" I asked.

Mrs. Carslake looked shocked.

"Oh really, Captain Norreys, she couldn't do a thing like *that*! Where could she go? She's no relations. I've sometimes thought that if a sympathetic young man came along—I don't feel, you know, that she has very strong principles. And she's quite good looking in a rather obvious sort of way."

"You don't like her very much, do you?" I said.

"Oh yes—I do—but of course I hardly know her. A vet —well, I mean it isn't like a doctor."

Having made this social distinction quite clear, Mrs. Carslake asked solicitously if there wasn't anything she could do for me.

"It's very kind of you. I don't think there's anything."

I was looking out of the window. She followed my eyes and saw what I was looking at.

"Oh," she said. "It's Isabella Charteris."

Together we watched Isabella coming nearer, passing through the field gate, coming up the steps to the terrace.

"She's quite a handsome girl," said Mrs. Carslake. "Very quiet, though. I often think these quiet girls are inclined to be sly."

The word sly made me feel indignant. I couldn't say anything because Mrs. Carslake had made her statement an exit line.

Sly—it was a horrible word! Especially as applied to Isabella. The quality most in evidence in Isabella was honesty—a fearless and almost painstaking honesty.

At least—I remembered suddenly the way she had let her scarf fall over those wretched tablets. The ease with which she had pretended to be in the middle of a conversation. And all without excitement or fuss—simply, naturally—as though she had been doing that sort of thing all her life.

Was that, perhaps, what Mrs. Carslake had meant by the word "sly"?

I thought to myself that I would ask Teresa what she thought about it. Teresa was not given to volunteering opinions, but if you asked for them you could have them.

When Isabella arrived, I saw that she was excited. I don't know that it would have been apparent to anybody else, but I spotted it at once. Up to a point, I was beginning to know Isabella fairly well.

She began abruptly without wasting time in greetings.

"Rupert is coming—really coming," she said. "He may arrive any day now. He's flying home, of course."

She sat down and smiled. Her long narrow hands were folded in her lap. Behind her head the yew tree outside made a pattern against the sky. She sat there looking beatific. Her attitude, the picture she made, reminded me of something. Something that I had seen or heard just lately. . . .

"Does his coming mean a lot to you?" I asked.

"Yes, it does. Oh yes." She added, "You see, I have been waiting a long time."

Was there possibly a touch of Mariana in the moated Grange about Isabella? Did she belong, just a little, to the Tennyson period?

"Waiting for Rupert?"

"Yes."

"Are you—so fond of him?"

"I think I am fonder of Rupert than anyone in the world." Then she added, managing somehow to give a different intonation to the repetition of the same words, "I —think I am."

"Aren't you sure?"

She looked at me with a sudden grave distress.

"Can one ever be sure of anything?"

It was not a statement of her feelings. It was definitely a question.

She asked me because she thought I might know the answer she did not know. She could not guess how that particular question hurt me.

"No," I said, and my voice was harsh in my own ears. "One can never be sure."

She accepted the answer, looking down at the quietness of her folded hands.

"I see," she said. "I see."

"How long is it since you have seen him?"

"Eight years."

"You are a romantic creature, Isabella," I said.

She looked at me questioningly.

"Because I believe that Rupert will come home and that we shall be married? But it isn't really romantic. It's more that it's a pattern—" Her long still hands quivered into life, tracing something on the surface of her frock. "My pattern and his pattern. They will come together and join. I don't think I could ever leave St. Loo. I was born here and I've always lived here. I want to go on living here. I expect I shall—die here."

She shivered a little as she said the last words, and at the same time a cloud came over the sun.

I wondered again in my own mind at her queer horror of death.

"I don't think you'll die for a long time, Isabella," I said consolingly. "You're very strong and healthy."

She assented eagerly.

"Yes, I'm very strong. I'm never ill. I think I might live to be ninety, don't you? Or even a hundred. After all, people do."

I tried to picture to myself an Isabella of ninety. I just couldn't see it. And yet I could easily imagine Lady St. Loo living to be a hundred. But then Lady St. Loo had a vigorous and forceful personality, she impinged on life, she was conscious of herself as a director and creator of events. She battled for life—Isabella accepted it.

Gabriel opened the door and came in, saying:

"Look here, Norreys—" and then stopped when he saw Isabella.

He said, "Oh—good morning, Miss Charteris."

His manner was slightly awkward and self-conscious. Was it, I wondered amusedly, the shadow of Lady St. Loo?

"We are discussing life and death," I said cheerfully. "I've just been prophesying that Miss Charteris will live to be ninety."

"I shouldn't think she'd want to," said Gabriel. "Who would?"

"I would," said Isabella.

"Why?"

She said, "I don't want to die."

"Oh," said Gabriel cheerfully, "nobody wants to die. At least they don't mind death, but they're afraid of dying. A painful messy business."

"It's death that I mind," said Isabella. "Not pain. I can stand a lot of pain."

"That's what you think," said Gabriel.

Something in his amused scornful tone angered Isabella. She flushed.

"I can stand pain."

They looked at each other. His glance was still scornful, hers was challenging.

And then Gabriel did something that I could hardly credit.

I had laid my cigarette down. With a quick gesture he leaned across me, picked it up and brought its glowing tip close to Isabella's arm.

She did not flinch or move her arm away.

I think I cried out in protest, but neither of them paid any attention to me. He pressed the glowing end down onto the skin.

The whole ignominy and bitterness of the cripple was mine at that moment. To be helpless, bound, unable to act.

I could do nothing. Revolted by Gabriel's savagery, I could do nothing to prevent it.

I saw Isabella's face slowly whiten with pain. Her lips closed tight. She did not move. Her eyes looked steadily into Gabriel's.

"Are you mad, Gabriel?" I cried. "What the hell do you think you're doing?"

He paid absolutely no attention to me. I might not have been in the room.

Suddenly, with a quick movement, he tossed the cigarette into the fireplace.

"I apologize," he said to Isabella. "You can take it all right."

And thereupon, without a further word, he went out of the room.

I was almost inarticulate, trying to get words out.

"The brute—the savage—what the hell did he think he was doing? He ought to be shot . . ."

Isabella, her eyes on the door, was slowly winding a handkerchief round her burnt arm. She was doing it, if I can use the term, almost absentmindedly. As though her thoughts were elsewhere.

Then, from a long way away, as it were, she looked at me.

She seemed a little surprised.

"What's the matter?" she asked.

I tried, incoherently, to tell her just what I felt about Gabriel's action.

"I don't see," she said, "why you should be so upset. Major Gabriel was only seeing if I could stand pain. Now he knows I can."

CHAPTER TWELVE

We had a tea-party that afternoon. A niece of Mrs. Carslake was staying in St. Loo. She had been at school with Isabella, so Mrs. Carslake told us. I had never been able to picture Isabella at school, so I agreed readily when Teresa suggested asking the niece, now a Mrs. Mordaunt, and Mrs. Carslake to tea. Teresa also asked Isabella.

"Anne Mordaunt is coming. I believe she was at school with you."

"There were several Annes," said Isabella vaguely. "Anne Trenchard and Anne Langley and Anne Thompson."

"I forget what her name was before she married. Mrs. Carslake did tell me."

Anne Mordaunt turned out to have been Anne Thompson. She was a lively young woman with a rather unpleasantly assertive manner. (Or, at any rate, that was my view.) She was in one of the Ministries in London, and her husband was in another Ministry, and she had a child who was conveniently parked somewhere where it wouldn't interfere with Anne Mordaunt's valuable contribution to the war effort.

"Though my mother seems to think that we might have Tony back now that the bombs are over. But really I do think a child in London is too difficult at present. The flat's so small, and one just can't get proper nannies, and there are meals, and of course I am out all day."

"I really think," I said, "that it was very public spirited of you to have a child at all when you have so much important work to do."

I saw Teresa, sitting behind the large silver tea tray, smile a little. She also, very gently, shook her head at me.

But my remark went down quite well with young Mrs. Mordaunt. In fact, it seemed to please her.

"One does feel," she said, "that one doesn't want to shirk any of one's responsibilities. Children are badly needed—especially in our class." She added, as a kind of afterthought, "Besides, I am absolutely devoted to Tony."

She then turned to Isabella and plunged into reminiscences of the old days at St. Ninian's. It seemed to me a conversation in which one of the two participants did not really know her part. Anne Mordaunt had to help her out more than once.

Mrs. Carslake murmured apologetically to Teresa:

"I'm so sorry Dick is late. I cannot think what is keeping him. He expected to be home by half-past four."

Isabella said, "I think Major Gabriel is with him. He passed along the terrace about a quarter of an hour ago."

I was surprised. I had not heard anyone pass. Isabella was sitting with her back to the window and could not possibly have seen anyone go by. I had had my eyes on her and she certainly had not turned her head or shown any awareness of anybody. Of course, her hearing was unusually quick, I knew that. But I wondered how she had known it was Gabriel.

Teresa said, "Isabella, I wonder if you would mind— no, please don't move, Mrs. Carslake—would you go along next door and ask them both if they wouldn't like to come and have some tea."

We watched Isabella's tall figure disappear through the doorway and Mrs. Mordaunt said:

"Isabella really hasn't changed at all. She's just the same. She always was the oddest girl. Walked about as though she were in a dream. We always put it down to her being so brainy."

"Brainy?" I said sharply.

She turned to me.

"Yes, didn't you know? Isabella's frightfully clever. Miss Curtis—the Head—was simply heartbroken because she wouldn't go on to Somerville. She matriculated when she was only fifteen and had several distinctions."

I was still inclined to think of Isabella as a creature charming to look at but not over gifted with brains. I still stared at Anne Mordaunt unbelievingly.

"What were her special subjects?" I asked.

"Oh, astronomy and mathematics—she was frightfully good at maths—and Latin and French. She could learn anything she put her mind to. And yet, you know, she just didn't care a bit. It quite broke Miss Curtis's heart. All Isabella seemed to want to do was to come back and settle down in this stuffy old Castle place."

Isabella came back with Captain Carslake and Gabriel.

The tea-party went with a swing.

"What is so bewildering to me, Teresa," I said later

that evening, "is the impossibility of ever knowing what any particular human being is really like. Take Isabella Charteris. That Mordaunt woman described her as brainy. I myself used to think she was practically a moron. Then again, I should have said that one of her special characteristics was honesty. Mrs. Carslake, however, says that she's sly. Sly! An odious word. John Gabriel says she's smug and stuck up. You—well, actually I don't know what you think—because you hardly ever say anything personal about people. But—well—what *is* the real truth of a human creature who can appear so differently to different people?"

Robert, who seldom joined in our conversations, moved restlessly and said rather unexpectedly:

"But isn't that just the point? People do appear differently to different people. So do things. Trees, for instance, or the sea. Two painters would give you an entirely different idea of St. Loo harbor."

"You mean one painter would paint it naturalistically and another symbolically?"

Robert shook his head rather wearily. He hated talking about painting. He never could find the words to express what he meant.

"No," he said. "They'd actually *see* it differently. Probably—I don't know—you pick out of everything the things in it which are significant to *you*."

"And one does the same to people, you think? But you can't have two diametrically opposite qualities. Take Isabella, she can't be brainy *and* a moron!"

"I think you're wrong there, Hugh," said Teresa.

"My dear Teresa!"

Teresa smiled. She spoke slowly and thoughtfully.

"You can have a quality and not use it. Not, that is, if you have a simpler method that gives the same results, or that—yes, that's more probable—costs you less trouble. The point is, Hugh, that we have, all of us, progressed such a long way from simplicity that we don't now know what it is when we meet it. To *feel* a thing is always much easier —much less trouble—than to *think* it. Only, in the complexities of civilized life, feeling isn't accurate enough.

"As an instance of what I mean, you know, roughly, if

asked, what time of day it is. Morning, midday—late afternoon—evening—you don't have to *think*—and you don't need, for that, accurate knowledge or any apparatus—sundials, water clocks, chronometers, watches or clocks. But if you have to keep appointments and catch trains and be at specific places at specific times, you do have to take thought and devise complicated mechanisms to provide accuracy. I think an attitude to life might be much the same. You feel happy, you are roused to anger, you like someone or something, you dislike someone or something, you feel sad. People like you and me, Hugh (but not Robert so much), *speculate* on what they feel, they *analyze* it, they *think* about it. They examine the whole thing and give themselves the *reason*. 'I am happy because of so and so—I like so and so because of so and so—I am sad today because of so and so.' Only, very often, they give themselves the wrong reasons, they willfully deceive themselves. But Isabella, I think, does not speculate—does not ask herself, ever, *why*. Because, quite frankly, she isn't interested. If you asked her to think—to tell you *why* she feels about something as she does feel, she could, I think, reason it out with perfect accuracy, and give you the correct answer. But she is like a person who has a good and expensive clock on the mantelpiece, but never winds it up because, in the kind of life she leads, it isn't important to know exactly what time it is.

"But at St. Ninian's she was asked to use her intellect, and she has got an intellect—but not, I should say, a particularly speculative intellect. Her bent is for mathematics, languages, astronomy. Nothing that requires imagination. We, all of us, use imagination and speculation as a means of escape—a way of getting outwards, away from ourselves. Isabella doesn't need to get away from herself. She can live with herself—she's in harmony with herself. She has no need for a more complex way of life.

"Possibly human beings were all like that in medieval times—even in Elizabethan days. I read in some book that a 'great man' in those days bore one meaning only—a person who had a big establishment, who was, quite simply, rich and powerful. It bore none of the spiritual and moral significance that we attach to it. The term had nothing to do with character."

"You mean," I said, "that people were direct and concrete in their attitude to life—they did not speculate much."

"Yes, Hamlet, with his musings, his 'to be or not to be,' was an entirely alien figure to his age. So much so that then and for long afterwards critics wrote condemning Hamlet as a play because of the fatal weakness of plot. 'There is no reason,' one of them said, 'why Hamlet should not kill the King in the first act. The only reason he does not do so is that if he had done, there would be no play!' It is quite unbelievable to them that there could be a play about character.

"But nowadays we are practically *all* Hamlets and Macbeths. We are all asking ourselves the whole time—" (her voice held suddenly a great weariness) " *'to be or not to be?'* Whether it is better to be alive or dead. Analyzing the successful as Hamlet analyzes (and envies!) Fortinbras.

"It is Fortinbras nowadays who would be the little understood figure. Moving ahead, confident, asking no questions of himself. How many of his sort are there in these days? Not many, I think."

"You think Isabella is a kind of female Fortinbras?" I asked smiling.

Teresa smiled too.

"Not so warlike. But direct of purpose and entirely single-minded. She would never ask herself, 'Why am I like I am? What do I really feel?' She knows what she feels and she is what she is." Teresa added softly, "And she will do—what she has to do."

"You mean she is fatalistic?"

"No. But for her I do not think there are ever alternatives. She will never see two possible courses of action—only one. And she will never think of retracing her steps, she will always go on. There's no backward way for the Isabellas. . . ."

"I wonder if there is any backward way for any of us!"
I spoke with bitterness.

Teresa said calmly, "Perhaps not. But there is usually, I think, a loophole."

"What do you mean exactly, Teresa?"

"I think one usually gets one chance of escape. . . . You don't usually realize it until afterwards . . . when you are looking back . . . but it's there . . ."

I was silent for a moment or two, smoking and thinking . . .

When Teresa had said that I had had a sudden vivid memory. I had just arrived at Caro Strangeways' cocktail party. I was standing in the doorway, hesitating a moment as my eyes accustomed themselves to the dim lamps and the haze of smoke. And there, at the far end of the room, I saw Jennifer. She didn't see me, she was talking to someone in her usual vivid animated way.

I was conscious of two sharply conflicting feelings. First a leap of triumph. I had known that we should meet again—and here was my instinctive knowledge proved true. That meeting in the train was not an isolated incident. I had always known it was not, and here was my belief being proved true. And yet—in spite of my excitement, my triumph—I had a sudden wish to turn round and leave the party . . . I had a wish to keep my meeting with Jennifer in the train as a single isolated happening—a happening that I should never forget. It was as though someone had said to me, "*That* was the best you could ever have of each other—a short space of perfection. Leave it like that."

If Teresa was right, that had been *my* "chance of escape . . ."

Well, I hadn't taken it. I had gone on. And Jennifer had gone on. And everything else had happened in sequence. Our belief in our mutual love, the lorry in the Harrow Road, my invalid chair, and Polnorth House. . . .

And brought back again, thus, to my original point of departure, my mind reverted to Isabella again, and I made a final protest to Teresa.

"But not sly, Teresa? Such an odious word. Not sly."

"I wonder," said Teresa.

"Sly? Isabella?"

"Isn't slyness the first—the easiest line of defence? Isn't

cunning one of the most primitive characteristics—the hare that crouches in her form—the grouse that flutters across the heather to distract you from her nest? Surely, Hugh, cunning is elemental. It's the only weapon you can use when you're helpless with your back to the wall."

She got up and moved towards the door. Robert had slipped off to bed already. With her fingers on the handle, Teresa turned her head.

"I believe," she said, "that you can really throw those tablets of yours away. You won't want them now."

"Teresa," I cried. "So you knew about them?"

"Of course I knew."

"But then—" I stopped. "Why do you say I shan't want them now?"

"Well, do you want them?"

"No," I said slowly. "You're right . . . I don't. I shall throw them away tomorrow."

"I'm so glad," said Teresa. "I've often been afraid . . ."

I looked at her curiously.

"Why didn't you try to take them away from me?"

She did not speak for a moment. Then she said:

"They've been a comfort to you, haven't they? They've made you feel secure—knowing that you always had a way out?"

"Yes," I said. "It's made a lot of difference."

"Then why are you so stupid as to ask why I didn't take them away from you?"

I laughed.

"Well, tomorrow, Teresa—they'll go down the drain-pipe. That's a promise."

"So at last you've begun to live again—to want to live."

"Yes," I said wonderingly. "I suppose I have. I really can't think why. But it's true. I'm actually interested in waking up tomorrow morning."

"You're interested, yes. I wonder who's responsible for that. Is it life in St. Loo? Or Isabella Charteris? Or John Gabriel?"

"It certainly isn't John Gabriel," I said.

"I'm not so sure. There's something about that man—"

"There certainly seems to be plenty of sex appeal!" I

said. "But he's the type I dislike—I can't stand a blatant opportunist. Why, that man would sell his grandmother if he saw a chance of making a profit out of her."

"I shouldn't be surprised."

"I wouldn't trust him an inch."

"No, he's not very trustworthy."

I went on, "He boasts. He's a flagrant publicity hound. He exploits himself and everybody else. Do you seriously think that that man is capable of one single disinterested action?"

Teresa said thoughtfully, "I think just possibly he might be—but if so, it would probably finish him for good."

I was to remember that remark of Teresa's within the next few days.

CHAPTER THIRTEEN

Our next local excitement was the whist drive. It was being got up by the Women's Institute.

It was being held where such affairs had always been held, in the Long Barn of Polnorth House. The Long Barn, I gather, was something rather special. Enthusiastic antiquarians came to gloat over it, measure it, photograph it, and write about it. It was considered in St. Loo as a kind of public possession. The inhabitants were proud of it.

There was a great hum of activity during the next two days. Organizing members of the Women's Institute drifted in and out.

I remained mercifully segregated from the main stream, but Teresa occasionally introduced what I can only describe as particularly choice specimens for my amusement and entertainment.

Since Teresa knew that I liked Milly Burt, Milly was admitted fairly frequently to my sitting room and we engaged together in various miscellaneous tasks such as writing out tickets, sticking or gumming decorations.

It was while we were engaged on these operations that I heard Milly's life story. As Gabriel had so brutally told me, I could only justify my existence by becoming a kind of ever-ready receiving set. I might be good for nothing else, but I was still good for that.

Milly Burt talked to me without self-consciousness— a kind of burbling self-revelation, like a gentle little stream.

She talked a great deal about Major Gabriel. Her hero worship where he was concerned had increased rather than diminished.

"What I think so wonderful about him, Captain Norreys, is that he's so *kind*. I mean when he's so busy and so rushed and has so many important things to do, yet he always remembers things and has such a nice teasing way of talking. I've never met anyone quite like him."

"You're probably right there," I said.

"With his wonderful war record and everything, he isn't a bit proud or stuck up—he's just as nice to me as to somebody important. He's nice to everybody—and he remembers about people and if their sons have been killed or if they're out in Burma or somewhere dreadful, and he always knows the right thing to say and how to make people laugh and cheer up. I don't know how he manages it all."

"He must have been reading Kipling's *If*," I said coldly.

"Yes. I'm sure he fills the unforgiving minute with sixty seconds' worth of distance run if anybody does."

"Probably a hundred and twenty seconds' worth," I suggested. "Sixty seconds wouldn't be enough for Gabriel."

"I wish I knew more about politics," said Milly wistfully. "I have read up all the pamphlets, but I'm not really good at canvassing or persuading people to vote. You see, I don't know the answers to the things they say."

"Oh well," I said consolingly, "all that sort of thing is just a knack. Anyway, to my mind canvassing is quite unethical."

She looked at me uncomprehendingly.

I explained:

"You shouldn't ever try to make people vote against their convictions," I said.

"Oh, I see—yes, I see what you mean. But we do think that the Conservatives are the only people who can finish off the war and make the peace the right way, don't we?"

"Mrs. Burt," I said, "what a really splendid little Tory you are. Is that what you say when you go canvassing?"

She blushed.

"No, I don't really know enough to talk about the political side. But I *can* say what a splendid man Major Gabriel is, and how sincere, and how it's people like him who are really going to matter."

Well, I thought to myself, that would be right down Gabriel's street . . . I looked into her flushed serious face. Her brown eyes were shining. I had an uncomfortable moment wondering whether perhaps a little more than hero worship was involved.

As though responding to my unexpressed thought, Milly's face clouded over.

"Jim thinks I'm an awful fool," she said deprecatingly.

"Does he? Why?"

"He says I'm such a fool I can't understand anything about politics—and anyway, the whole thing's a racket. And he says what the—I mean he says I can't possibly be any use, and if I go round talking to people it's as good as a vote for the other side from everyone I talk to. Captain Norreys, do you think that's true?"

"No;" I said firmly.

She brightened up.

"I know I'm stupid in some ways. But it's only when I'm rattled, and Jim always can rattle me. He likes upsetting me. He likes—" She stopped. Her lips were quivering.

Then suddenly she scattered the white slips of paper she was working on and began to cry—deep heart-rending sobs.

"My dear Mrs. Burt—" I said helplessly.

What the hell can a man do who lies helpless in an invalid chair? I couldn't pat her shoulder. She wasn't near enough. I couldn't push a handkerchief into her hand. I couldn't mutter an excuse and sidle out of the room. I couldn't even say, "I'll get you a cup of tea."

No, I had to fulfill my function, the function which,

as Gabriel had been kind (or cruel) enough to tell me, was the only one left to me. So I said, helplessly, "My dear Mrs. Burt—" and waited.

"I'm so unhappy—so terribly unhappy—I see now—I should never have married Jim."

I said feebly, "Oh, come now, it's not so bad as that, I'm sure."

"He was so gay and so dashing—and he made such nice jokes. He used to come round to see the horses if anything went wrong. Dad kept a riding school, you know. Jim looks wonderful on a horse."

"Yes—yes."

"And he didn't drink so much then—at least perhaps he did, but I didn't realize it. Though I suppose I ought to have realized it, because people came and talked about it to me. Said he lifted his elbow too much. But you see, Captain Norreys, I didn't believe it. One doesn't, does one?"

"No," I said.

"I thought he would give all that up when we were married. I'm sure he didn't drink at all while we were engaged. I'm *sure* he didn't."

"Probably not," I said. "A man is capable of anything when he's courting."

"And they said he was cruel, too. But that I didn't believe. Because he was so sweet to me. Although I did see him once with a horse—he'd lost his temper with it—he was punishing it—" She gave a little quick shiver and half closed her eyes. "I felt—I felt quite differently—just for a moment or two. 'I'm not going to marry you if that's the sort of man you are,' I said to myself. It was funny, you know—I felt suddenly as though he was a stranger—not my Jim at all. It would have been funny if I had broken it off, wouldn't it?"

Funny was not what she really meant, but we agreed that it would have been funny—and also very fortunate.

Milly continued, "But it all passed over—Jim explained, and I realized that every man does lose his temper now and then. It didn't seem important. You see, I thought that I'd make him so happy that he'd never want to drink or lose his temper. That's really why I wanted to marry him so much—to make him happy."

"To make anyone happy is not the real purpose of marriage," I said.

She stared at me.

"But surely, if you love anyone, the first thing you think about is to make them happy?"

"It is one of the more insidious forms of self-indulgence," I said. "And fairly widespread. It has probably caused more unhappiness than anything else in matrimonial statistics."

She still stared. I quoted to her those lines of Emily Brontë's sad wisdom:

> "I've known a hundred ways of love
>   And each one made the loved one rue."

She protested, "I think that's *horrid*!"

"To love anyone," I said, "is always to lay upon that person an almost intolerable burden."

"You do say funny things, Captain Norreys."

Milly seemed almost disposed to giggle.

"Pay no attention to me," I said. "My views are not orthodox, only the result of sad experience."

"Oh, have you been unhappy too? Do you—"

I shied from the awakening sympathy in her eyes. I steered the conversation back to Jim Burt. It was unfortunate for Milly, I thought, that she had been the gentle easily browbeaten type—the worst type for marriage with a man like Burt. From what I heard of him, I guessed that he was the type of man who likes spirit in both horseflesh and women. An Irish termagant might have held him and aroused his unwilling respect. What was fatal for him was to have power over an animal or a human being. His sadistic disposition was fed by his wife's flinching fear of him, and her tears and sighs. The pity of it was that Milly Burt (or so at least I thought) would have made a happy and successful wife to most men. She would have listened to them, flattered them, and made a fuss over them. She would have increased their self-esteem and good humor.

She would, I thought suddenly, have made John Gabriel a good wife. She might not have advanced his ambitions (but was he really ambitious? I doubted it) but she would have assuaged in him that bitterness and self-distrust that now and then showed through the almost insufferable cocksureness of his manner.

James Burt, it seemed, combined jealousy with neglect, as is by no means uncommon. Railing at his wife for her poor spiritedness and stupidity, he yet resented violently any signs of friendship shown her by another man.

"You wouldn't believe it, Captain Norreys, but he even said horrible things about Major Gabriel. Just because Major Gabriel asked me to have morning coffee at the Ginger Cat last week. He was so nice—Major Gabriel, I mean, not Jim—and we sat on there a long time, although I'm sure he couldn't really spare the time—and talking so nicely, asking me about Dad and the horses and about how things used to be at St. Loo then. He couldn't have been nicer! And then—and then—to have Jim say the things he did—and get in one of his rages—he twisted my arm—I got away and locked myself in my room. I'm terrified of Jim sometimes . . . Oh, Captain Norreys—I'm so dreadfully unhappy. I do wish I was dead."

"No, you don't, Mrs. Burt, not really."

"Oh, but I *do*. What's going to happen to me? There's nothing to look forward to. It'll just go on getting worse and worse . . . Jim's losing a lot of his practice because of drinking. And that makes him madder than ever. And I'm frightened of him. I really am frightened . . ."

I soothed her as best I could. I did not think things were quite as bad as she made out. But she was certainly a very unhappy woman.

I told Teresa that Mrs. Burt led a very miserable life, but Teresa did not seem much interested.

"Don't you want to hear about it?" I asked reproachfully.

Teresa said, "Not particularly. Unhappy wives so resemble each other that their stories get rather monotonous."

"Really, Teresa!" I said. "You are quite inhuman."

"I admit," said Teresa, "that sympathy has never been my strong point."

"I have an uneasy feeling," I said, "that the wretched

little thing is in love with Gabriel."

"Almost certainly, I should say," said Teresa drily.

"And you're still not sorry for her?"

"Well—not for that reason. I should think that to fall in love with Gabriel would be a most enjoyable experience."

"Really, Teresa! You're not in love with him yourself, are you?"

No, Teresa said, she wasn't. Fortunately, she added.

I pounced on that and told her she was illogical. She had just said that to fall in love with John Gabriel would be enjoyable.

"Not to me," said Teresa. "Because I resent—and have always resented—feeling emotion."

"Yes," L said thoughtfully. "I believe that's true. But why? I can't understand that."

"And I can't explain."

"Try," I urged.

"Dear Hugh, how you like to probe! I suppose because I have no instinct for living. To feel that my will and my brain can be entirely swamped and overriden by emotion is insufferable to me. I can control my actions and to a large extent my thoughts—not to be able to control my emotions is galling to my pride—it humiliates me."

"You don't think there is really any danger of anything between John Gabriel and Mrs. Burt, do you?" I asked.

"There has been some talk. Carslake is worried about it. Mrs. Carslake says there is a lot of gossip going about."

"That woman! She would."

"She would, as you say. But she represents public opinion. The opinion of the malicious gossipy strata of St. Loo. And I understand Burt's tongue has wagged rather freely when he's had a couple—which is very often. Of course he's known to be a jealous husband and a lot of what he says is discounted, but it all causes talk."

"Gabriel will have to be careful," I said.

"Being careful isn't quite his line of country, is it?" said Teresa.

"You don't think he really cares for the woman?"

Teresa considered before she replied, "I think he's very sorry for her. He's a man easily moved to pity."

"You don't think he'd get her to leave her husband? That would be a disaster."

"Would it?"

"My dear Teresa, it would bust up the whole show."

"I know."

"Well, that would be fatal, wouldn't it?"

Teresa said in an odd voice, "For John Gabriel? Or for the Conservative Party?"

"I was really thinking of Gabriel," I said. "But for the Party too, of course."

"Of course, I'm not really politically minded," said Teresa. "I don't care in the least if one more Labour Member gets elected to Westminster—though it would be too awful if the Carslakes heard me say so. What I am wondering is, if it would be a disaster for John Gabriel or not? Suppose it resulted in his being a happier man?"

"But he's frightfully keen on winning the election," I exclaimed.

Teresa said that success and happiness were two entirely different things.

"I don't really believe," she said, "that they ever go together."

CHAPTER FOURTEEN

On the morning of the whist drive, Captain Carslake came and unburdened himself of a great deal of alarm and despondency.

"There's nothing *in* it," he said. "Of course there's nothing *in* it! I've known little Mrs. Burt all my life. She's *quite* all right—very strictly brought up and all that—a thoroughly nice little woman. But you know what people's minds are."

I knew what his wife's mind was. It was probably his criterion for judging other people's.

He continued walking up and down and rubbing his

nose in an exasperated fashion.

"Gabriel's a good-natured chap. He's been nice to her. But he's been careless—you can't afford to be careless during an election."

"What you really mean is you can't afford to be kind."

"Exactly—exactly. Gabriel's been too kind—kind in public. Having morning coffee with her at the Ginger Cat café. It doesn't look well. Why should he have coffee with her there?"

"Why shouldn't he?"

Carslake ignored that.

"All the old cats are there having their elevenses at that time. Then I believe he walked quite a long way with her in the town the other morning—he actually carried her shopping bag for her."

"A Conservative gentleman could do no less," I murmured.

Carslake still paid no attention to my remarks.

"And he gave her a lift in his car one day—out by Sprague's farm it was. Quite a long way out. Made it look as though they'd been off together for an outing."

"After all, this is nineteen forty-five not eighteen forty-five," I said.

"Things haven't altered much down here," said Carslake. "I don't mean the new bungalows and the arty crowd —they're up-to-date, no morals to speak of—but they'll vote Labour anyway. It's the solid respectable old-fashioned part of the town that we've got to worry about. Gabriel will really have to be more careful."

Half an hour later I had Gabriel burst in upon me in a white heat of indignation. Carslake had made tactful representations to him and the result had been the usual result of tactful words spoken in season.

"Carslake," he said, "is a foul minded old woman! Do you know what he's had the cheek to say to me?"

"Yes," I said. "I know all about it. And by the way, this is the time of day when I rest. I don't have visitors."

"Nonsense," said Gabriel. "You don't need to rest. You're perpetually resting. You've got to listen to what I have to say about this. Damn it, I've got to let off steam to someone, and as I told you the other day, it's about all you're good for, and you might as well make up your mind to listen gracefully to people when they want to hear the sound of their own voices!"

"I remember the particularly charming way you put it," I said.

"I really said it because I wanted to get under your skin."

"I knew that."

"I suppose it was rather a brutal thing to say, but after all, it's no good your being thin-skinned."

"Actually," I said, "your saying it rather bucked me up. I've been so wrapped in consideration and tactfulness that to hear a little plain speaking was quite a relief."

"You're coming on," said Gabriel, and went on unburdening himself about his own affairs.

"Can't I offer an unhappy girl a cup of coffee in a public café without being suspected of immorality?" he demanded. "Why should I pay any attention to what people think who have minds like a public sewer?"

"Well, you want to be an M.P., don't you?" I said.

"I'm going to be an M.P."

"Carslake's point is that you won't be one, if you parade your friendship with Mrs. Burt."

"What damned swine people are!"

"Oh yes, yes!"

"As if politics isn't the dirtiest racket there is!"

"Again, yes, yes."

"Don't grin, Norreys. I find you damned annoying this morning. And if you think there's anything there shouldn't be between me and Mrs. Burt, you're wrong. I'm sorry for her, that's all. I've never said a word to her that her husband or the whole Watch Committee of St. Loo couldn't overhear if they wanted to. My God, when you think of the way I've held myself in where women are concerned! And I *like* women!"

He was deeply injured. The matter had its humorous side.

He said earnestly, "That woman's terribly unhappy. You don't know—you can't guess what she's had to put up with. How brave she's been. And how loyal. And she doesn't complain. Says she feels it must be partly her fault somehow. I'd like to get my hands on Burt—he's an unutterable brute. His own mother wouldn't recognize him when I'd done with him!"

"For Heaven's sake," I cried, really alarmed. "Haven't you got any prudence, Gabriel? A public row with Burt and your chances of the election would be dished."

He laughed and said, "Who knows? It might be worth it. I'll tell you—" He stopped.

I looked to see what had stopped the flow. It was Isabella. She had just come in through the window. She said good morning to us both, and said Teresa had asked her to come over and help arrange the Barn for tonight.

"You are going to honor us with your presence, I hope, Miss Charteris?" said Gabriel.

His speech held a mixture of oiliness and sprightliness that did not at all become him. Isabella always seemed to have a bad effect on him.

She said, "Yes." She added, "We always come to these things."

Then she went off in search of Teresa and Gabriel exploded.

"Very kind of the Princess," he said. "Very condescending. Nice of her to mix with the common herd! So gracious! I tell you, Norreys, Milly Burt is worth a dozen stuck up girls like Isabella Charteris. Isabella Charteris! Who is she, after all?"

It seemed obvious who Isabella was. But Gabriel enjoyed himself developing the theme.

"Poor as a church mouse. Living in a ruined tumbledown old castle and pretending to be grander than anybody else. Hanging about there twiddling her fingers and doing nothing and hoping that the precious heir will come home and marry her. She's never seen him and she can't care a button for him, but she's willing to marry him. Oh yes. Faugh! These girls make me sick. Sick, Norreys. Pampered Pekinese dogs, that's what they are. Lady St. Loo, that's what she means to be. What the hell is the good of being Lady St. Loo nowadays? All that kind of thing is over and done with. Comic, that's all it is nowadays—a music hall joke—"

"Really, Gabriel," I said. "You are undoubtedly in the wrong camp. You'd make a magnificent speech on Wilbraham's platform. Why don't you change places?"

"To a girl like that," said Gabriel, still breathing hard, "Milly Burt is just the vet's wife! Someone to be condescended to at political beanfeasts—but not to be asked to tea at the Castle—oh no, not good enough for *that!* I tell you Milly Burt's worth six of Isabella Stuck Up Charteris."

I closed my eyes with determination.

"Could you go away, Gabriel?" I said. "No matter what you say, I am still a very sick man, and I insist on having my rest. I find you extremely tiring."

CHAPTER FIFTEEN

Everybody had a word to say on the subject of John Gabriel and Milly Burt, and everybody said it, sooner or later, to me. My room, in the throes of preparation for the whist drive, became a kind of Green Room. People repaired there for cups of tea or glasses of sherry. Teresa could, of course, have barred them out, but she did nothing of the kind, and I was glad that she didn't for I found myself deeply interested in this rapidly woven pattern of hearsay and malice and obscure jealousy.

Between Milly Burt and John Gabriel there existed, of that I was sure, nothing that could be taken exception to. Friendliness and pity on his side, adoring hero worship on hers.

Yet I realized, reluctantly, that implicit in the present position were the further developments that malicious hearsay had anticipated. Technically innocent, Milly Burt was already more than half in love with Gabriel whether she knew it herself or not. Gabriel was essentially a man of sensual appetites. At any moment protective chivalry might be transformed into passion.

I thought that but for the exigencies of the election,

their friendship might already have turned into a love affair. Gabriel, I suspected, was a man who needed to be loved and at the same time admired. The black subterranean venom in him could be appeased so long as he could cherish and protect. Milly Burt was the kind of woman who needed to be cherished and protected.

I thought cynically to myself that it would be one of the better kinds of adulteries—based less on lust than on love, pity, kindness, and gratitude. Still, it would, undoubtedly, be adultery and a large proportion of the voting electorate of St. Loo would see it as adultery without extenuating circumstances, and would forthwith record votes for the desiccated Mr. Wilbraham of blameless private life, or else sit at home and refrain from voting at all. Rightly or wrongly, Gabriel was fighting this election on personal appeal—the votes recorded would be given for John Gabriel not for Winston Churchill. And John Gabriel was skating on thin ice.

"I know I oughtn't to mention such a thing perhaps," Lady Tressilian said breathlessly. She had been walking fast. She undid her gray flannel coat and sipped gratefully at tea served in one of the late Miss Amy Tregellis' Rockingham cups. She dropped her voice in a conspiratorial manner. "But I wonder if anyone has said anything to you about—about Mrs. Burt and—and our candidate."

She looked at me like a spaniel in distress.

"I'm afraid," I said, "that people have been talking a little."

Her nice face looked very worried.

"Oh dear," she said. "I wish they wouldn't. She's very nice, you know, very nice indeed. Not at all the type that —I mean, it's so unfair. Of course, if there were anything in it, anything to be careful about—why, then they would be careful and no one would know anything about it. It's just because it's quite all right and there's nothing to conceal that they haven't, well—thought—"

Mrs. Bigham Charteris stumped in energetically at this point. She was full of indignation about some horse or other.

"Disgraceful carelessness," she said. "That man Burt

is absolutely unreliable. He's drinking more and more—and now it's beginning to show in his work. Of course, I've always known he was hopeless with dogs, but he did pull himself together over horses and cows—the farmers all swear by him—but now I hear that Polneathy's cow died calving—just due to negligence. And now Bentley's mare. Burt will do for himself if he's not careful."

"I was just talking to Captain Norreys about Mrs. Burt," said Lady Tressilian. "Asking if he'd heard anything—"

"All a pack of nonsense," said Mrs. Bigham Charteris robustly, "but these things stick. Now people are saying that *that's* the reason Burt's drinking so much. More stuff and nonsense. He drank too much and knocked his wife about long before Major Gabriel ever came to this place.

"Still," she added, "something's got to be done about it. Somebody's got to speak to Major Gabriel."

"Carslake has mentioned the matter to him, I believe," I said.

"That man's got no tact," said Mrs. Bigham Charteris. "I suppose Gabriel flew right off the handle?"

"Yes," I said. "He did."

"Gabriel's a damned fool," said Mrs. Bigham Charteris. "Soft-hearted—that's his trouble. H'm—somebody had better speak to *her*. Give her a hint to keep out of the way until after the election. I don't suppose she's the least idea what people are saying." She turned on her sister-in-law. "You'd better do it, Agnes."

Lady Tressilian turned purple and bleated miserably:

"Oh really, Maud—I shouldn't know what to say. I'm sure I'm *quite* the wrong person."

"Well, we mustn't risk letting Mrs. Carslake do it. That woman's just poison."

"Hear, hear," I said, with feeling.

"And I've a shrewd suspicion that she's at the bottom of a lot of the talk herself."

"Oh, surely not, Maud. She wouldn't do anything to prejudice our own candidate's chances."

"You'd be surprised, Agnes," said Mrs. Bigham Charteris darkly, "at what I've seen go on in a regiment. If a woman wants to be spiteful it seems to override everything else—her husband's chances of promotion—*everything*. If you ask me," she went on, "she'd have liked a mild flirtation with John Gabriel herself!"

"Maud!"

"Ask Captain Norreys what he thinks. He's been on the spot, and lookers-on see most of the game, they say."

Both ladies looked at me expectantly.

"I certainly don't think——" I began—and then changed my mind. "I think you're perfectly right," I said to Mrs. Bigham Charteris.

The significance of some of Mrs. Carslake's half-finished remarks and glances had suddenly dawned on me. I thought it possible that, unlikely as it seemed, Mrs. Carslake had not only taken no steps to scotch any flying rumors, but might actually have secretly encouraged them.

It was, I reflected, an unpleasant world.

"If anyone's going to tackle Milly Burt, I think Captain Norreys is the person," said Mrs. Bigham Charteris unexpectedly.

"No," I cried.

"She likes you and an invalid is always in rather a privileged position."

"Oh, I do so agree," said Lady Tressilian delighted at a suggestion which released her from an unpleasant task.

"*No!*" I said.

"She's decorating the Barn now," said Mrs. Bigham Charteris rising energetically. "I'll send her along—tell her there's a cup of tea waiting for her."

"I shan't do anything of the kind," I cried.

"Oh yes, you will," said Mrs. Bigham Charteris, who had not been a colonel's wife for nothing. "We've all got to do *something* to prevent those dreadful Socialists from getting in."

"It's to help dear Mr. Churchill," said Lady Tressilian. "After all he's done for the country."

"Now that he's won the war for us," I said, "he ought to sit back and write his history of the war (he's one of the best writers of our times) and have a nice rest while Labour mismanages the peace."

Mrs. Bigham Charteris had gone energetically through the window. I continued to address Lady Tressilian.

"Churchill deserves a rest," I said.

"Think of the terrible mess Labour would make of things," said Lady Tressilian.

"Think of the terrible mess anyone will make of it," I said. "Nobody can help making a mess of things after a war. Don't you think, really, that it had better not be our side? Anyway," I added frantically as I heard footsteps and voices outside, *"you're* obviously the person to hint things to Milly Burt. These things come better from another woman."

But Lady Tressilian was shaking her head.

"No," she said. "They don't—they don't really. Maud is quite right. You're the right person. I'm sure she'll understand."

The last pronoun referred, I presumed, to Milly Burt. I myself had very grave doubts whether she would understand.

Mrs. Bigham Charteris brought Milly Burt into the room like a naval destroyer convoying a merchant ship.

"Here you are," she said breezily. "There's the tea. Pour out a cup and sit down and amuse Captain Norreys. Agnes, I want you. What did you do with the prizes?"

The two women swept out of the room. Milly Burt poured out her cup of tea and came to sit down by me. She looked a little bewildered.

"There isn't anything wrong, is there?" she asked.

Perhaps if she had not used that opening phrase I should have shirked the task imposed upon me. As it was, the opening made it slightly easier for me to say what I had been told to say.

"You're a very nice person, Milly," I said. "Do you ever realize that a lot of people aren't particularly nice?"

"What do you mean, Captain Norreys?"

"Look here," I said. "Do you know that there's a lot of ill-natured talk going on about you and Major Gabriel?"

"About me and Major Gabriel?" She stared at me. A slow burning blush suffused her face up to the roots of the hair. It embarrassed me and I averted my eyes. "You mean that it's not only Jim—that outside people say so too—that they really think—?"

"When an election is on," I said, hating myself, "the prospective candidate has to be particularly careful. He has, in St. Paul's words, to avoid even the appearance of evil. . . . You see? Silly little things like having coffee with him at the Ginger Cat or his meeting you in the street and carrying your parcels, are quite enough to set people off."

She looked at me with wide frightened brown eyes.

"But you do believe, don't you, that there's never been *anything*, that he's never said a word? That's he's been just very very kind? That's all! *Really*, that's all."

"Of course, I know that. But a prospective candidate can't even afford to be kind. Such," I added bitterly, "is the purity of our political ideals."

"I wouldn't do him any harm," said Milly. "Not for the world."

"I'm sure you wouldn't."

She looked at me appealingly.

"What can I do to—to put things right?"

"I should simply suggest that you—well, keep out of his way until the election's over. Try not to be seen together in public if you can help it."

She nodded quickly.

"Yes, of course. I'm ever so grateful to you for telling me, Captain Norreys. I should never have thought of it. I—he's been so wonderful to me—"

She got up and everything would have ended very satisfactorily if John Gabriel had not chosen that moment to come in.

"Hullo," he said. "What's going in here? I've just come from a meeting, been talking till my throat's hoarse. Got any sherry? I'm visiting some mothers next—and whiskey isn't too good on the breath."

"I must be off now," said Milly. "Goodbye, Captain Norreys. Goodbye, Major Gabriel."

Gabriel said, "Wait a moment. I'll walk home with you."

"No. No, please. I—I must hurry."

He said, "All right. I'll sacrifice the sherry then."

"Please!" She was flushed, embarrassed. "I don't want you to come. I—I want to go alone."

She almost ran from the room. Gabriel wheeled round on me.

"Who's been saying things to her? You?"

"I have," I said.

"What do you mean by butting into my affairs?"

"I don't care a damn about your affairs. This is the affair of the Conservative Party."

"And do you care a damn about the Conservative Party?"

"When I actually come to think of it, no," I admitted.

"Then why do the Nosey Parker?"

"If you want to know, it's because I like little Mrs. Burt, and if she were to feel later that you had lost the election from any reason connected with your friendship for her, she would be very unhappy."

"I shan't lose the election through my friendship with her."

"It's quite possible that you might, Gabriel. You underestimate the force of prurient imagination."

He nodded.

"Who put you up to talking to her?"

"Mrs. Bigham Charteris and Lady Tressilian."

"Those old hags! And Lady St. Loo?"

"No," I said. "Lady St. Loo had nothing to do with it."

"If I thought *she* was issuing orders," said Gabriel, "I'd take Milly Burt away for the weekend and to hell with the lot of them!"

"That would finish things very nicely!" I said. "I thought you wanted to win this election?"

He grinned suddenly, his good temper restored.

"I'll win it all right," he said.

CHAPTER SIXTEEN

That evening was one of the loveliest evenings of the whole summer. People flocked along to the Long Barn.

There was fancy dress and dancing as well as the whist drive proper.

Teresa wheeled me along to have a look at the scene. Everyone seemed very animated. Gabriel was in good form, telling stories, mixing with the crowd, quick with back chat and repartee. He looked particularly cheerful and confident. He seemed to be paying special attention to the ladies present, rather exaggerating his manner to them. I thought that was astute of him. His infectious good spirits made themselves felt—and everything was going with a swing.

Lady St. Loo, gaunt and impressive, was there to set things in motion. Her presence was taken as a compliment. I had discovered that she was both liked and feared. She was a woman who did not hesitate to speak her mind on occasions—on the other hand, her kindness, though unspectacular, was very real, and she took a keen interest in the town of St. Loo and its vicissitudes.

"The Castle" was much respected. When the billeting officer had been tearing his hair over the difficulties of placing evacuees early in the war, an uncompromising message had arrived from Lady St. Loo. Why had she not been allocated any evacuees?

To Mr. Pengelley's halting explanations that he had been unwilling that she should be troubled—some of the children were very undisciplined—she had replied:

"Naturally we shall do our share. We can easily take five children of school age, or two mothers with families, whichever you prefer."

The mothers and families had not been a success. The two London women had been terrified of the long echoing stone passages of the Castle, they had shivered and murmured about ghosts. When the gales blew from the sea the inadequate heating set them huddling together with their teeth chattering. The place was a nightmare to them after the cheery warmth and humanity of a London tenement. They soon departed and were replaced with children of school age to whom the Castle was one of the most exciting things that had ever happened. They climbed about its ruins, hunted insatiably for a rumored underground passage, and enjoyed the echoing corridors inside. They submitted to being mothered by Lady Tressilian, were awed and fascinated by Lady St. Loo, were taught not to fear horses and dogs by Mrs. Bigham Charteris, and got on excellent terms with the old Cornish cook who made them saffron buns.

Later Lady St. Loo twice made representations to the billeting officer. Certain children had been placed on lonely farms—the farmers in question were not, according to her, either kindly or trustworthy. She insisted on inquiries being made. It was found that in one case the children were being badly underfed. In the other they were adequately fed but dirty and neglected.

It all heightened the respect in which the old lady was held. The Castle wouldn't stand for things being done wrong, people said.

Lady St. Loo did not grace the whist drive with her presence too long. She and her sister and sister-in-law departed together. Isabella remained on to help Teresa, Mrs. Carslake and other ladies.

I myself stayed watching it all for about twenty minutes. Then Robert pushed my chair back to the house. I stopped him on the terrace. It was a warm night and the moonlight was magnificent.

"I'll stay out here," I said.

"Right. Do you want a rug or anything?"

"No, it's quite warm."

Robert nodded. He turned on his heel and strode back to the Barn where he had undertaken certain tasks.

I lay there smoking peacefully. The Castle was silhouetted against the moonlit sea and looked more than ever like a stage property. A hum of music and voices came from the direction of the Barn. Behind me the house was dark and shuttered save for one open window. A freak of the moonlight made it look as though a causeway of light stretched from the Castle to Polnorth House.

Along it, I pleased myself by imagining, rode a figure in shining armor—young Lord St. Loo returned to his home . . . A pity that battle-dress was so much less romantic than chain mail.

At variance with the far off human noises from the Barn came the thousand and one noises of the summer night, small creakings and rustlings—tiny animals creeping about their lawful occasions, leaves stirring, the faint far off hoot of an owl. . . .

Vague contentment stole over me. It was true what I had told Teresa—I was beginning to live again. The past and Jennifer were like a brilliant unsubstantial dream—between it and me was the morass of pain and darkness and lethargy from which I was only now emerging. I could not take up my old life—the break was clean. The life that I was beginning was a new life. What was this new life of mine going to be? How was I going to shape it? Who and what was the new Hugh Norreys? I felt interest beginning to stir. What did I know? What could I hope? What was I going to do?

I saw a tall white clad figure come out from the Long Barn. It hesitated a moment then walked in my direction. I had known at once it was Isabella. She came and sat down on the stone bench. The harmony of the night was complete.

We were quite a long time without saying anything. I was very happy. I didn't want to spoil it by talking. I didn't even want to think.

It was not till a sudden breeze sprang up off the sea and ruffled Isabella's hair so that she raised her arm to her head that the spell was broken. I turned my head to look at her. She was staring, as I had stared earlier, at the moonlit causeway leading to the Castle.

"Rupert ought to come tonight," I said.

"Yes." There was a tiny catch in her voice. "He ought."

"I've been picturing his arrival," I said, "in chain mail on a horse. But really, I suppose, he'll come in battle-dress and a beret."

"He must come soon," Isabella said. "Oh, he *must* come soon . . ."

There was urgency, almost distress, in her voice.

I didn't know what was in her mind, but I felt vaguely alarmed for her.

"Don't set your heart too much on his coming," I warned

her. "Things have a knack of turning out all wrong."

"I suppose they do, sometimes."

"You expect something," I said, "and it isn't there. . . ."

Isabella said, "Rupert must come *soon*."

There was distress, real urgency in her voice.

I would have asked her what she meant, but at that moment John Gabriel came out of the Long Barn and joined us.

"Mrs. Norreys sent me along to see if there was anything you wanted," he said to me. "Like a drink?"

"No, thank you."

"Sure?"

"Quite sure."

He more or less ignored Isabella.

"Fetch yourself one," I said.

"No, thanks. I don't want one." He paused and then said, "Lovely night. On such a night did young Lorenzo etcetera etcetera."

We were all three silent. Music came faintly from the Long Barn. Gabriel turned to Isabella.

"Would you care to come and dance, Miss Charteris?"

Isabella rose and murmured in her polite voice, "Thank you. I would like to very much."

They walked away together rather stiffly without saying anything to each other.

I began to think about Jennifer. I wondered where she was and what she was doing. Was she happy or unhappy? Had she found, as the phrase goes, "someone else?" I hoped so. I hoped so very much.

There was no real pain in thinking about Jennifer, because the Jennifer that I had once known had not really existed. I had invented her to please myself. I had never bothered about the real Jennifer. Between her and me there had stood the figure of Hugh Norreys caring for Jennifer.

I remembered vaguely as a child going carefully and unsteadily down a big flight of stairs. I could hear the faint echo of my own voice saying importantly, "Here's Hugh going downstairs . . ." Later, a child learns to say *"I."* But somewhere, deep inside himself, that "I" doesn't penetrate. He goes on being not "I" but a spectator. He sees himself in a series of pictures. I had seen Hugh comforting Jennifer, Hugh being all the world to Jennifer, Hugh going to make Jennifer happy, going to make up to Jennifer for all that had happened to her.

Yes, I thought to myself suddenly, just like Milly Burt. Milly Burt deciding to marry her Jim, seeing herself making him happy, curing him of drinking, not caring, really, to acknowledge the real Jim.

I tried this process on John Gabriel. Here's John Gabriel, sorry for the little woman, cheering her up, being kind to her, helping her along.

I switched to Teresa. Here's Teresa marrying Robert, here's Teresa—

No, that wouldn't work. Teresa, I thought to myself, was adult—she had learnt to say "*I*."

Two figures came out from the Barn. They did not come towards me. Instead they turned the other way down the steps to the lower terrace and the water garden. . . .

I pursued my mental researches. Lady Tressilian, seeing herself persuade me back to health, to interest in life. Mrs. Bigham Charteris seeing herself as the person who always knew the right way to tackle things, still in her own eyes the efficient wife of the Colonel of the regiment. Well, why the hell not? Life is hard, and we must have our dreams.

Had Jennifer had dreams? What was Jennifer really like? Had I ever bothered to find out? Hadn't I seen always what I wanted to see, my loyal unhappy wonderful Jennifer?

What was she really? Not so very wonderful, not so very loyal (when one came to think of it!), certainly unhappy . . . determinedly unhappy. I remembered her remorse, her self-accusations when I had lain there, a broken and shattered wreck. Everything was *her* fault, her doing. What did that mean after all but Jennifer seeing herself in a tragic rôle?

Everything that has happened must have been caused by Jennifer. This is Jennifer, the tragic, the unhappy figure, for whom everything goes wrong, and who takes the blame for everything that goes wrong with everyone else. Milly

Burt, probably, would do much the same. Milly—my thoughts switched abruptly from theories of personality to present everyday problems. Milly hadn't come tonight. Perhaps that was wise of her. Or would her absence cause equal comment?

I shivered suddenly and gave a start. I must have been nearly asleep. It was getting much colder . . .

I heard steps coming up from the lower terrace. It was John Gabriel. He walked towards me and I noticed that he walked unsteadily. I wondered if he had been drinking.

He came up to me. I was startled at his appearance. His voice when he spoke was thick, the words were slurred. He presented every appearance of a man who had been drinking, but it was not alcohol that had got him into this state.

He laughed, a drunken sort of laugh.

"That girl!" he said. "That girl! I told you that girl was just like any other girl. Her head may be in the stars, but her feet are set in clay all right."

"What are you talking about, Gabriel?" I said sharply. "Have you been drinking?"

He let out another laugh.

"That's a good one! No, I haven't been drinking. There are better things to do than drink. A proud stuck up bit of goods! Too much of a fine lady to associate with the common herd! I've shown her where she belongs. I've pulled her down from the stars—I've shown her what she's made of, common earth. I told you long ago she wasn't a saint— not with a mouth like that. . . . She's human all right. She's just like all the rest of us. Make love to any woman you like, they're all the same . . . all the same!"

"Look here, Gabriel," I said furiously, "what have you been up to?"

He let out a cackle of laughter.

"I've been enjoying myself, old boy," he said. "That's what I've been doing, enjoying myself. Enjoying myself in my own way—and a damned good way too."

"If you've insulted that girl in any way—"

"Girl? She's a full grown woman. She knows what she's

doing, or she ought to know. She's a woman all right. Take my word for it."

Again he laughed. The echo of that laugh haunted me for many years. It was a gross materialistic chuckle, horribly unpleasant. I hated him then and I went on hating him.

I was horribly conscious of my own helplessness, my immobility. He made me conscious of it by his swift contemptuous glance. I can imagine no one more odious than John Gabriel was that night . . .

He laughed again and went unsteadily towards the Barn. I looked after him full of angry rage. Then, while I was still revolving the bitter pill of my invalid status I heard someone coming up the terrace steps. Lighter, quieter footfalls this time.

Isabella came up onto the terrace and across towards me and sat down on the stone bench by my side.

Her movements, as always, were assured and quiet. She sat there in silence as she had sat earlier in the evening. Yet I was conscious, distinctly conscious, of a difference. It was as though, without outward sign, she sought reassurance. Something within her was startled and awake. She was, I felt certain, in deep trouble of spirit. But I did not know, I could not even guess, what exactly was passing through her mind. Perhaps she did not know herself.

I said, rather incoherently, "Isabella, my dear—is it all right?"

I did not quite know what I meant.

She said presently, "I don't know . . ."

A few minutes later she slipped her hand into mine. It was a lovely trustful gesture, a gesture I have never forgotten. We did not say anything. We sat there for nearly an hour. Then the people began to come out of the Long Barn and various women came and chatted and congratulated each other on the way everything had gone, and one of them took Isabella home in her car.

It was all dreamlike and unreal.

CHAPTER SEVENTEEN

I expected that Gabriel would keep away from me next day, but Gabriel was always unaccountable. He came into my room just before eleven o'clock.

"Hoped I'd find you alone," he said. "I suppose I made the most thundering fool of myself last night."

"You can call it that. I should call it something stronger. You're an unutterable swine, Gabriel."

"What did she say?"

"She didn't say anything."

"Was she upset? Was she angry? Damn it all, she must have said *something*. She was with you almost an hour."

"She didn't say anything at all," I repeated.

"I wish to God I'd never—" He stopped. "Look here, you don't think I seduced her, do you? Nothing of that kind. Good Lord, no. I only—well—I only made love to her a bit, that's all. Moonlight, a pretty girl—well, I mean it might have happened to anybody."

I didn't answer. Gabriel answered my silence as if it had spoken words.

"You're right," he said. "I'm not particularly proud of myself. But she drove me mad. She's driven me mad ever since I met her. Looking as though she was too holy to be touched. That's why I made love to her last night—yes, and it wasn't pretty lovemaking either—it was pretty beastly. But she responded, Norreys . . . She's human all right—as human as any little piece you pick up on a Saturday night. I daresay she hates me now. I've not slept a wink—"

He walked violently up and down. Then he asked again:

"Are you sure she didn't say anything? Anything at all?"

"I've told you twice," I said coldly.

He clutched his head. It might have been a funny gesture, but it was actually purely tragic.

"I never know what she thinks," he said. "I don't know

anything about her. She's somewhere where I can't get at her. It's like that damned frieze at Pisa. The blessed, sitting there in Heaven under the trees, smiling. I *had* to drag her down—I had to! I couldn't stand it any more. I tell you I just couldn't stand it. I wanted to humble her, to drag her down to earth, to see her look ashamed. I wanted her down in Hell with me—"

"For God's sake, Gabriel, shut up," I said angrily. "Haven't you any decency?"

"No, I haven't. You wouldn't have if you'd been through what I've been through. All these weeks. I wish I'd never seen her. I wish I could forget her. I wish I didn't know she existed."

"I'd no idea—"

He interrupted me.

"*You* wouldn't have any idea. You never do see an inch in front of your nose! You're the most selfish individual I've ever met, entirely wrapped up in your own feelings. Can't you see that I'm licked? A little more of this and I shan't care whether I get into Parliament or not."

"The country," I said, "may be the gainer."

"The truth is," said Gabriel gloomily, "that I've made the most unholy hash of everything."

I did not reply. I had stood so much from Gabriel in his boastful moods, that I was able to take a certain amount of satisfaction in seeing him thoroughly cast down.

My silence annoyed him. I was glad. I had meant it to annoy him.

"I wonder, Norreys, if you have any idea how smug and puritanical you look? What do you think I ought to do —apologize to the girl—say I lost my head—something like that?"

"It's nothing to do with me. You've had so much experience with women that you ought to know."

"I've never had anything to do with a girl like that before. Do you think she's shocked—disgusted? Does she think I'm a complete swine?"

Again I found pleasure in telling him what was the simple truth—that I did not know what Isabella thought or felt.

"But I think," I said, looking through the window, "that she's coming here now."

Gabriel went very red in the face and his eyes took on a hunted look.

He took up his position in front of the fireplace, an ugly position, his legs straddled, his chin thrust forward. He had a hangdog sheepish look that sat very ill upon him. It gave me pleasure to observe that he looked common and furtive and mean.

"If she looks at me as though I were something the cat had brought in—" he said, but did not finish the sentence.

Isabella, however, did not look at him as though he were something the cat had brought in. She said good morning, first to me and then to him. Her manner made no difference between us. It was, as usual, grave and perfectly courteous. She had the serene and untouched look that she always had. She had brought a message for Teresa and when she learned Teresa was next door with the Carslakes she went in search of her, giving us both a small gracious smile as she left the room.

When she had shut the door behind her Gabriel began to swear. He cursed her steadily and vitriolically. I tried to stem the torrent of his malice but without avail. He shouted at me:

"Hold your tongue, Norreys. This has nothing to do with you. I tell you I'll get even with that proud stuck-up bitch if it's the last thing I ever do."

And with that he charged out of the room, banging the door behind him so that Polnorth House shook with the impact.

I did not want to miss Isabella on her way back from the Carslakes so I rang my bell and had my chair pushed out onto the terrace.

I had not long to wait. Isabella came out of the far French window and along the terrace towards me. With her usual naturalness she came straight to the stone seat and sat down. She did not say anything. Her long hands were, as usual, loosely folded on her lap.

Usually I was content enough, but today my speculative mind was active. I wanted to know what went on in that rather nobly shaped head. I had seen the state that Gabriel was in. I had no idea what impression, if any, had been left on Isabella by the happenings of the preceding evening. The difficulty of dealing with Isabella was that you had to put things into plain words—to proffer any accepted euphemisms merely resulted in her giving you a stare of blank bewilderment.

Yet custom being what it is, my first remark was completely ambiguous.

"Is it all right, Isabella?" I asked.

She turned her level inquiring gaze on me.

"Gabriel," I said, "is upset this morning. I think he wants to apologize to you for what happened last night."

She said, "Why should he apologize?"

"Well—" I said, hesitating, "he thinks he behaved rather badly."

She looked thoughtful and said, "Oh, I see."

There was no trace of embarrassment in her manner. My curiosity drove me on to ask further questions, notwithstanding the fact that the whole subject was no business of mine.

"Don't *you* think he behaved badly?" I asked.

She said, "I don't know . . . I simply don't know . . ." She added, in a faintly apologetic manner, "You see, it's something I simply haven't had time to think about."

"You weren't shocked, or frightened, or upset?"

I was curious, really curious.

She seemed to turn over my words in her mind. Then she said, still with that air of viewing something with detachment that was a long way off:

"No, I don't think so. Ought I to have been?"

And there, of course, she turned the tables on me. Because I didn't know that answer. What ought a normal girl to feel when she first meets—not love—certainly not tenderness—but the easily awakened passion of a man of somewhat gross disposition?

I had always felt (or had I only wanted to feel?) that there was something extraordinarily virginal about Isabella. But was that really so? Gabriel, I remembered, had twice mentioned her mouth. I looked at that mouth now. The underlip was full—it was almost a Hapsburg mouth— it was unpainted—a fresh natural red—yes, it was a sensuous—a passionate mouth.

Gabriel had wakened response in her. But what was that response? Purely sensual? Instinctive? Was it a response to which her judgment assented?

Then Isabella asked me a question. She asked me quite simply if I liked Major Gabriel.

There were times when I would have found it hard to answer that question. But not today. Today I was quite definite in my feelings about Gabriel.

I said, uncompromisingly, "No."

She said thoughtfully, "Mrs. Carslake doesn't like him either."

I disliked a good deal being bracketed with Mrs. Carslake.

I, in my turn, asked a question.

"Do you like him, Isabella?"

She was silent for a very long time. And when words did struggle to the surface, I realized that they had arisen from a deep morass of bewilderment.

"I don't know him . . . I don't know anything about him. It's terrible when you can't even talk to anyone."

It was difficult for me to understand what she meant because always, where I had been attracted towards women, understanding had been, as it were, the lure. The belief (sometimes an erroneous belief) in a special sympathy between us. The discovery of things we both liked, things we disliked, discussions of plays, of books, of ethical points, of mutual sympathies or mutual aversions.

The sensation of warm comradeship had always been the start of what was quite frequently not comradeship at all, but merely camouflaged sex.

Gabriel, according to Teresa, was a man attractive to women. Presumably Isabella had found him attractive—but if so his male attractiveness was a bald fact to her—it was not disguised by a veneer of spurious understanding. It was as a stranger, an alien, that he came. But did she really find him attractive? Was it possibly his lovemaking that she found attractive and not the man himself?

These, I perceived, were all speculations. And Isabella did not speculate. Whatever her feelings toward Gabriel, she would not analyze them. She would accept them—accept them as a woven part of Life's tapestry, and go on to the next portion of the design.

And it was that, I suddenly realized, that had aroused Gabriel's almost maniacal rage. For a split second I felt a stirring of sympathy for him.

Then Isabella spoke.

She asked me in her serious voice why I thought it was that red roses never lasted in water.

We discussed the question. I asked her what her favorite flowers were.

She said red roses and very dark brown wallflowers and what she called thick-looking pale mauve stocks.

It seemed to me rather an odd selection. I asked her why she liked those particular flowers. She said she didn't know.

"You've got a lazy mind, Isabella," I said. "You know perfectly well if only you'd take the trouble to think."

"Would I? Very well, then, I will think."

She sat there, upright and serious, thinking. . . .

(And that, when I remember Isabella, is how I see her—and always shall see her to the end of time. Sitting in the sunlight on the upright carved stone seat, her head proud and erect, her long narrow hands folded peacefully on her lap and her face serious, thinking of flowers.)

She said at last, "I think it is because they all look as though they would be lovely to touch—rich—like velvet. . . . And because they have a lovely smell. Roses don't look right growing—they grow in an ugly way. A rose wants to be by itself, in a glass—then it's beautiful—but only for a very short time—then it droops and dies. Aspirin and burning the stems and all those things don't do any good—not to red roses—they're all right for the others. But nothing keeps big dark red roses long—I wish they didn't die."

It was quite the longest speech Isabella had ever made

to me. She was more interested in talking about roses than she had been in talking about Gabriel.

It was, as I have said, a moment I shall always remember. It was the climax, you see, of our friendship. . . .

From where my chair was placed, I faced the footpath across the fields from St. Loo Castle. And along that footpath a figure was approaching—a figure in battle-dress and a beret. With a sudden pang that astonished me, I knew that Lord St. Loo had come home.

CHAPTER EIGHTEEN

Sometimes one has the illusion of a certain series of events having happened a wearisome number of times before. I had that impression as I watched young Lord St. Loo coming towards us. It seemed to me that again and again and again I had lain here, helpless, immobile, watching Rupert St. Loo coming across the fields . . . It had happened often before, it would happen again . . . it would happen throughout Eternity.

Isabella, my heart said, *this is goodbye.* This is Fate coming for you.

It was the fairy story atmosphere again; it was illusion, unreality. I was going to assist at the familiar end of a familiar story.

I gave a little sigh as I looked at Isabella. She was quite unaware of Fate approaching. She was looking down at her long narrow white hands. She was still thinking of roses— or possibly of very dark brown wallflowers . . .

"Isabella," I said gently. "Someone is coming . . ."

She looked up, without haste, mildly interested. She turned her head. Her body went rigid, then a little tremor went through it.

"Rupert," she said . . . "Rupert. . . ."

It mightn't, of course, have been Rupert at all. Nobody could have told at that distance. But it was Rupert.

He came, a little hesitantly, through the gate and up the

steps to the terrace, a faintly apologetic air about him. Because Polnorth House belonged to strangers whom he hadn't yet met. . . . But they had told him, at the Castle, that he would find his cousin there.

Isabella rose to her feet as he came up onto the terrace and she took two steps towards him. He quickened his own steps towards her.

She said, "Rupert . . ." very softly as they met.

He said, "Isabella!"

They stood there together, their hands clasped, his head bent just a little protectively.

It was perfect—quite perfect. If it had been a film scene there would have been no necessity for a retake . . . On the stage, it would have brought a lump to the throat of any romantic playgoing woman over middle age. It was idyllic—unreal—a fairy story's happy ending. It was Romance with a capital R.

It was the meeting of a boy and girl who had been thinking of each other for years, each building up an image that was partly illusory, and finding when they at last came together, that miraculously the illusion was at one with reality. . . .

It was the sort of thing which doesn't happen, one says, in real life. But it was happening, here before my eyes.

They settled things, really, in that first moment. Rupert had always held tenaciously, in the back of his mind, to the determination to come back to St. Loo and marry Isabella. Isabella had always had the calm certainty that Rupert would come home and marry her, and that they would live together at St. Loo . . . happy ever after.

And now, for both of them, their faith was justified and the vision was fulfilled.

Their moment didn't last long. Isabella turned to me. Her face was shining with happiness.

"This is Captain Norreys," she said. "My cousin Rupert."

St. Loo came forward and shook hands with me and I took a good look at him.

I still think that I have never seen anyone handsomer. I don't mean that he was of the "Greek God" type. His was an entirely virile and masculine beauty. A lean weatherbeaten brown face, a rather large moustache, deep blue eyes, a head perfectly set on broad shoulders, narrow flanks, and well shaped legs. His voice was attractive, deep and pleasant. He had no Colonial accent. There was humor in his face, intelligence, tenacity, and a certain calm stability.

He apologized for coming across informally like this, but he had just arrived by air, and had come straight across country from the aerodrome by car. On arrival, he had been told by Lady Tressilian that Isabella had gone over to Polnorth House and that he would probably find her there.

He looked at Isabella as he finished speaking and a twinkle came into his eye.

"You've improved a lot from a schoolgirl, Isabella," he said. "I remember you with immensely long spindly legs, two flapping plaits, and an earnest air."

"I must have looked terrible," said Isabella thoughtfully.

Lord St. Loo said he hoped he would meet my sister-in-law and my brother whose paintings he admired very much.

Isabella said that Teresa was with the Carslakes and she would go and tell her. Did Rupert want the Carslakes too?

Rupert said he didn't want the Carslakes, and he couldn't remember them anyway, even if they had been here when he was last at St. Loo as a schoolboy.

"I expect, Rupert," said Isabella, "that you will have to have them. They will be very excited about your coming. Everyone will be excited."

Young Lord St. Loo looked apprehensive. He had only got a month's leave, he said.

"And then you have to go back to the East?" asked Isabella.

"Yes."

"And after the Japanese war is over—will you come back here then, to live?"

She asked him the question with gravity. His face too became grave.

"It depends," he said, "on several things. . . ."

There was a little unexplained pause . . . it was as though both of them were thinking of the same things. There was already full harmony and understanding between them.

Then Isabella went away in search of Teresa, and Rupert St. Loo sat down and began to talk to me. We talked shop and I enjoyed it. Since I had come to Polnorth House I had lived perforce in a feminine atmosphere. St. Loo was one of those pockets in a country which remain consistently out of the war. Their connection with it is only by hearsay, gossip and rumors. Such soldiers as there are about are soldiers on leave who want to leave their war mentality behind them.

I had been plunged, instead, into a purely political world—and the political world, at any rate in places like St. Loo, is essentially female. It is a world of calculation of effects, of persuasion, of a thousand small subtleties, coupled with that large amount of sheer uninteresting drudgery that is, again, the female quota to existence. It is a world in miniature—the outside universe of bloodshed and violence has its place only as a stage backcloth might have its place. Against the background of a world war not yet terminated we were engaged in a parochial and intensely personal struggle. The same thing was going on all over England camouflaged by noble clichés. Democracy, Freedom, Security, Empire, Nationalisation, Loyalty, Brave New World—those were the words, the banners.

But the actual elections, as I began to suspect was always the case, were swayed by those personal insistencies which are so much greater, so much more urgent, than the Words and Names—the Banners—under which the fight is enrolled.

Which side will give me a house to live in? Which side will bring my boy Johnnie, my husband David back from overseas? Which side will give my babies the best chance in the future? Which side will keep further wars from taking and killing my man, and perhaps my sons?

Fine words butter no parsnips. Who will help me to reopen my shop? Who will build me a house? Who will give us all more food, more clothing coupons, more towels, more soap?

*Churchill's all right. He won the war for us. He saved
us from having the Germans here. I'll stick by Churchill.
Wilbraham's a schoolmaster. Education's the thing to
get children on in the world. Labour will give us more
houses. They say so. Churchill won't bring the boys home
as quickly. Nationalise the mines—then we'll all have coal.*

*I like Major Gabriel. He's a real man. He cares about
things. He's been wounded, he's fought all over Europe, he
hasn't stayed at home in a safe job. He knows what we feel
about the boys out there. He's the kind we want—not a
blasted schoolmaster. School teachers! Those evacuated
teachers wouldn't even help Mrs. Polwidden to wash up
the breakfast things. Stuck-up, that's what they are.*

What are politics after all but adjacent booths at the
world's fair, each offering their own cheap-jack specific to
cure all ills? . . . And the gullible public swallows the
chatter.

That was the world I had lived in since I returned to
life and began living it once more. It was a world I had
never known before, a world entirely new to me.

At first I had despised it indulgently. I had character-
ized it to myself as just another racket. But now I was beginning to realize on what it was based, what passionate
realities, what endless struggling hopes for survival. The
woman's world—not the man's. Man was still the hunter—
carefree, ragged, often hungry, pushing ahead, a woman
and a child at his tail. No need for politics in *that* world,
only the quick eyes, the ready hand, the stalking of the
prey.

But the civilized world is based on earth, earth that
grows and produces. That is a world that erects buildings,
and fills them with possessions—a maternal, fecund world
where survival is infinitely more complicated and may suc-
ceed and fail in a hundred different ways. Women do not
see the stars, they see the four walls of a shelter from the
wind, the cooking pot on the hearth, the faces of well-fed
children asleep.

I wanted—badly—to escape from that female world.
Robert was no help to me—he was a painter. An artist, ma-
ternally concerned with the bringing forth of new life.

Gabriel was masculine enough—his presence had cut welcomely across the infinitesimal web of intrigue—but essentially he and I were out of sympathy.

With Rupert St. Loo, I was back in my own world. The world of Alamein and Sicily, of Cairo and Rome. We talked the old language, in the old idiom, discovering mutual acquaintances. I was back again, a whole man, in the wartime careless world of imminent death, good cheer, and physical enjoyment.

I liked Rupert St. Loo enormously. He was, I felt sure, a first class officer, and he had an extremely attractive personality. He had brains, good humor, and a sensitive intelligence. He was the kind of man, I thought, who was needed to build up the new world. A man with traditions and yet with a modern and forward-looking mind.

Presently Teresa came and joined us, with Robert, and she explained how we were engaged in a fury of electioneering, and Rupert St. Loo confessed that he wasn't much of a politician: and then the Carslakes came in with Gabriel, and Mrs. Carslake gushed, and Carslake put on his hearty manner, and was delighted to see Lord St. Loo, and this was our candidate Major Gabriel.

Rupert St. Loo and Gabriel greeted each other pleasantly and Rupert wished him luck and talked a little about the campaign and how things were going. They stood together outlined against the sunlight, and I noted the contrast, the really cruel contrast, between them. It wasn't only that Rupert was handsome and Gabriel was an ugly little man—it went deeper than that. Rupert St. Loo was poised, assured. He had a naturally courteous and kindly manner. You felt, too, that he was dead straight. A Chinese merchant, if I may put it that way, would have trusted him to take away any amount of goods without paying for them—and the Chinese merchant would have been right. Gabriel showed up badly against the other—he was nervous, too assertive, he straddled his legs and moved about uneasily. He looked, poor devil, rather a nasty common little man—worse, he looked the kind of man who would be honest as long as it paid him. He was like a dog of doubtful ancestry that has got along all right until it is brought into the show ring side by side with a thoroughbred.

Robert was standing by my couch, and I drew his attention to the two men with a mumbled word.

He caught my meaning and looked thoughtfully at them both. Gabriel was still weaving uneasily from foot to foot. He had to look up at Rupert as they talked, and I don't think he liked having to do that.

Someone else was watching the two men—Isabella. Her eyes seemed at first to look at them both and then, unmistakably, they focused on Rupert. Her lips parted, she threw back her head proudly, a little color crept up in her cheeks. That proud glad look of hers was a lovely thing to see.

Robert noticed her attitude by a quick glance. Then his eyes returned thoughtfully to Rupert St. Loo's face.

When the others went in for drinks, Robert stayed on the terrace—I asked him what he thought of Rupert St. Loo. His answer was a curious one.

"I should say," he said, "that there wasn't a single bad fairy at his christening."

CHAPTER NINETEEN

Well, Rupert and Isabella didn't take long to settle things. My own opinion is that it had been settled that very first moment when they met on the terrace by my chair.

There was, I think, an agonized relief on the part of both of them that the dream each had cherished secretly for so long had not let them down when it came to the testing.

For as Rupert told me, some days later, he had cherished a dream.

We had become fairly intimate, he and I. He, too, was glad of male society. The atmosphere of the Castle was overloaded with feminine adoration. The three old ladies doted openly on Rupert, even Lady St. Loo herself dropped some of her own particular astringent quality.

So Rupert liked coming across and talking to me.

"I used to think," he said abruptly one day, "that I was a damned fool about Isabella. It's curious, say what you like, to make up your mind you're going to marry someone—when that someone is a child—and a scraggy child at that—and then find you don't change your mind."

I told him that I had known of similar cases.

He said thoughtfully, "The truth of it is, I suppose, that Isabella and I belong . . . I've felt always that she's a part of me, a part that I couldn't get hold of yet, but that I'd have to get hold of some day to make things complete. Funny business. She's an odd girl."

He smoked a minute or two in silence and then said:

"I think what I like best about her is that she's got no sense of humor."

"You don't think she has?"

"None whatever. It's wonderfully restful . . . I've always suspected that a sense of humor is a kind of parlor trick we civilized folk have taught ourselves as an insurance against disillusionment. We make a conscious effort to see things as funny, simply because we suspect they are unsatisfactory."

Well, there was something in that. . . . I thought about it with a slightly wry smile. . . . Yes, Rupert St. Loo had got something there.

He was staring out at the Castle. He said jerkily:

"I love that place. I've always loved it. Yet I'm glad I was brought up in New Zealand until the time I came over to Eton. It's given me detachment. I can see the place from outside, as well as identifying myself with it without reflection. To come here from Eton for holidays, to know it was really mine, that someday I should live here—to recognize it, as it were, as something I had always wanted to have . . . to have the feeling—the first time I saw it—a queer eerie feeling—of coming home.

"And Isabella was part of it. I was sure then and have been ever since that we would marry and live here for the rest of our mortal lives." His jaw set grimly. "And we *will* live here! In spite of taxation, and expenses and repairs—and the threat of land nationalisation. That is our home, Isabella's and mine."

They were officially engaged on the fifth day after Rupert's return.

It was Lady Tressilian who told us the news. It would be in the *Times* tomorrow, or the day after, she said, but she wanted us to hear of it first. And she was so very *very* happy about it all!

Her nice round face was quivering with sentimental pleasure. Both Teresa and I felt touched by her happiness. It showed so clearly the lack of certain things in her own life. In the joy of the moment, she became far less maternal in her attitude to me which made me enjoy her company a great deal better. For the first time she brought me no booklets and hardly tried at all to be bright and encouraging. It was clear that Rupert and Isabella occupied all her thoughts.

The attitudes of the other two old ladies varied slightly. Mrs. Bigham Charteris redoubled her energy and briskness. She took Rupert on immense walks around the estate, introduced him to his tenants and lectured him on roofs and repairs and what had positively got to be done, and what could and indeed must, be left undone.

"Amos Polflexen always grouses. He had entirely new pointing to the walls two years ago. Something must be done about Ellen Heath's chimney. She's been very patient. The Heaths have been tenants of the estate for three hundred years."

But it was Lady St. Loo's attitude that I found the most interesting. For some time I could not understand it. Then one day I got the clue. It was triumph. A curious sort of triumph—a kind of gloating as over a battle won against an invisible and non-existent antagonist.

"It will be all right now," she said to me.

And then she gave a sigh—a long tired sigh. It was as though she said, *"Lord, now lettest thou thy servant depart in peace . . ."* She gave me the impression of one who has been afraid—but has not dared to show fear—and who knows the occasion for fear is now over.

Well, I suppose that the odds against young Lord St. Loo returning and marrying a cousin he had not seen for eight years were pretty heavy. Far the most likely thing was for Rupert to have married a stranger in the war years. Marriages take place quickly in war time. Yes, it must have been long odds against Rupert marrying Isabella.

And yet there was a rightness about it—a fitness.

I asked Teresa if she did not agree and she nodded her head thoughtfully.

"They're a wonderful pair," she said.

"Made for each other. That's what old family servants say at weddings, but this time it really is true."

"It *is* true. It's incredible . . . Don't you feel sometimes, Hugh, as though you'll wake up?"

I considered a moment or two because I knew what she meant.

"Nothing to do with St. Loo Castle is real," I said.

I was bound to hear John Gabriel's opinion. He kept up his habit of frankness with me. As far as I could make out, Gabriel disliked Lord St. Loo. That was natural enough, because Rupert St. Loo necessarily stole a good deal of Gabriel's thunder.

The whole of St. Loo was thrilled by the arrival of the Castle's rightful owner. The original inhabitants were proud of the antiquity of his title and remembered his father. The new inhabitants were more snobbishly thrilled.

"Disgusting lot of sheep," said Gabriel. "It's amazing to me how, say what they will, the Englishman always loves a title."

"Don't call a Cornishman an Englishman," I said. "Haven't you learnt that yet?"

"It slipped out. But it's true, isn't it? Either they come fawning round—or else they go to the other extreme and say what a farce the whole thing is and get violent, and that's just inverted snobbery."

"What about your feelings?" I said.

Gabriel immediately grinned. He was always appreciative of a point that told against him.

"I'm an inverted snob all right," he said. "The thing I'd

really like better than anything in the world would be to have been born Rupert St. Loo."

"You astonish me," I said.

"There are some things you've got to be born with— I'd give anything to have his legs," said Gabriel thoughtfully.

I remembered what Lady Tressilian had said at Gabriel's first meeting, and it interested me to see what a perceptive person Gabriel was.

I asked whether Gabriel felt Rupert St. Loo was stealing his thunder?

Gabriel considered the question seriously on its merits without showing any signs of annoyance.

No, he said, he thought it was quite all right because Lord St. Loo wasn't his political opponent. It was all additional propaganda for the Conservative Party.

"Though I daresay if he *did* stand—I mean if he *could* stand (which of course he can't, being a peer) he'd be quite likely to stand for Labour."

"Surely not," I objected. "Not as a landowner."

"He wouldn't like land nationalisation, of course—but things are very twisted round nowadays, Norreys. Farmers and solid working-class men are the staunch Conservatives —and young men with intellects and degrees and lots of money are Labour, mainly, I suppose, because they don't know the first thing about really working with their hands and haven't an idea what a working man really wants."

"And what does the working man want?" I asked, because I knew Gabriel was always giving one different answers to this question.

"He wants the country to be prosperous—so that *he* can be prosperous. He thinks the Conservatives are more likely to make the country prosperous because they know more about money, which of course is really very sound. I should say Lord St. Loo is really an old-fashioned Liberal —and of course nobody's got any use for a Liberal. No, they haven't, Norreys, it's no use your opening your mouth to say what you're going to say. You wait for the result of the elections. The Liberals will have diminished so much that you'll have to look for them with a magnifying glass.

Nobody ever does like Liberal ideas, really, by which I mean that nobody ever likes the middle course. It's too damned tame."

"And you consider Rupert St. Loo is an advocate of the middle way?"

"Yes. He's a reasonable man—keeps in with the old and welcomes the new—in fact, neither fish, flesh, nor good red herring. Gingerbread—that's what he is!"

"What?" I demanded.

"You heard what I said. Gingerbread! Gingerbread castle! Gingerbread owner of castle." He snorted. "Gingerbread wedding!"

"And a gingerbread bride?" I asked.

"No. She's all right . . . she's just strayed in—like Hansel and Gretel into the gingerbread house. It's attractive, gingerbread, you can break off a bit of it and eat it. It's edible all right."

"You don't like Rupert St. Loo much, do you?"

"Why should I? Come to that, he doesn't like me."

I considered for a moment or two. No, I did not think Rupert St. Loo did like John Gabriel.

"Still, he'll have to have me," said Gabriel. "Here I shall be—member of Parliament for his part of the world. They'll have to ask me to dinner from time to time and he'll sit on platforms with me."

"You're very sure of yourself, Gabriel. You're not in yet."

"I tell you the thing's a certainty. It's *got* to be. I shouldn't get another chance, you know. I'm by way of being an experiment. If the experiment fails, my name's mud and I'm done for. I can't go back to soldiering, either. You see, I'm not an administrative soldier—I'm only useful when there's a real scrap on. When the Japanese war ends, I'm finished. Othello's occupation's gone."

"I have never," I said, "found Othello a credible character."

"Why not? Jealousy never is credible."

"Well, shall we say—not a sympathetic character. One isn't sorry for him. One feels he is merely a damned fool."

"No," said Gabriel reflectively. "No—one isn't sorry

for him. Not sorry for him in the way one is sorry for Iago."

"Sorry for Iago? Really, Gabriel, you seem to have the oddest sympathies."

He flashed me a queer look.

"No," he said. *"You* wouldn't understand."

He got up and walked about, moving jerkily. He pushed some of the things on the writing table about unseeingly. I saw with some curiosity that he was laboring under some deeply felt inarticulate emotion.

"I understand Iago," he said. "I understand even why the poor devil never says anything in the end except

> *Demand me nothing; what you know, you know.*
> *From this time forth, I never will speak word.*

He turned on me. "Fellows like you, Norreys, fellows who've lived on good terms with yourself all your life, who've been able to grow up with yourself without flinching (if I can put it like that) well, what the hell can you know about the Iagos—the doomed men, the little mean men? My God, if I ever produced Shakespeare, I'd go to town on Iago—I'd get an actor who was an actor—an actor who could move you to the bowels! Imagine to yourself what it's like to be born a coward—to lie and cheat and get away with it—to love money so much that you wake up and eat and sleep and kiss your wife with money foremost in your brain. And all the time to *know* what you are. . . .

"That's the hell of life—to have one good fairy at the christening in amongst all the bad ones. And when the rest of the crew have turned you into a dirty skunk, to have Fairy Daydream wave her wand and flute out, 'I give him the gift of seeing and knowing. . .'

" 'We needs must love the highest when we see it.' What damned fool said that? Wordsworth, probably—a man who couldn't even see a primrose and be satisfied with the lovely thing . . .

"I tell you, Norreys, you hate the highest when you see it—hate it because it's not for you—because you can never be what you'd sell your soul to be. The man who really values courage is often the man who runs away when danger comes. I've seen that, more than once. Do you think a man is what he wants to be? A man is what he is born. Do you think the poor devil who worships money wants to worship money? Do you think the man with a sensual imagination wants to have a sensual imagination? Do you think the man who runs away wants to run away?

"The man you envy (really envy) isn't the man who's done better than you. The man you envy is the man who *is* better than you.

"If you're down in the mud, you hate the human being who's up amongst the stars. You want to pull her down . . . down . . . down . . . to where you're wallowing in your pigsty . . . pity Iago, I say. He'd have been all right if he hadn't met Othello. He'd have got along very well doing the confidence trick. Nowadays he'd have been selling non-existent goldmining shares to chumps in the Ritz Bar.

"A plausible fellow, Iago, so honest, always able to take in the simple soldier. Nothing easier than to take in a soldier—the greater the soldier, the more of a fool he is in business matters. It's always soldiers who buy dud shares, and believe in schemes for getting up Spanish treasure from sunk galleons, and buy chicken farms that are on their last legs. Soldiers are the believing kind. Othello was the kind of mug who would have fallen for any plausible tale put across by an artist—and Iago was an artist. You've only got to read between the lines in that play and it's as clear as day that Iago's been embezzling the regimental funds. Othello doesn't believe that—oh no, not honest stupid Iago —it's just muddleheadedness on the dear old fellow's part —but he gets in Cassio and puts him in over Iago's head. Cassio was a countercaster and that's an accountant or I'll eat my hat. A good honest fellow, Iago (so Othello thought), but not bright enough for promotion.

"Remember all that swashbuckling stuff Iago spouts about his prowess in battles? All hooey, Norreys—it never happened. It's what you can hear any day in a pub from the man who was never near the front line. Falstaff stuff, only this time it's not comedy but tragedy. Iago, poor devil,

wanted to be an Othello. He wanted to be a brave soldier
and an upright man, and he couldn't be, any more than a
hunchback can stand upright. He wanted to cut a dash
with women, and women hadn't any use for him. That
good-natured trollop of a wife of his despised him as a man.
She was only too ready to hop into bed with other men.
You bet all the women wanted to go to bed with Othello!
I tell you, Norreys, I've seen some odd things happen with
men who are sexually shamed. It turns them pathological.
Shakespeare knew. Iago can't open his mouth without a
stream of black, thwarted, sexual venom pouring out of it.
What nobody ever seems to see is, that that man suffered!
He could see beauty—he knew what it was—he knew a
noble nature. My God, Norreys, material envy, envy of
success, of possessions, of riches—is nothing—nothing at
all to spiritual envy! That's vitriol all right—eating in, de-
stroying you. You see the highest, and against your will you
love it, and so you hate it, and you don't rest till you have
destroyed it—till you've torn it down and stamped it out
. . . Yes, Iago suffered, poor devil . . .

"And if you ask me, Shakespeare knew that and was
sorry for the poor wretch. In the end, I mean. I daresay he
started out dipping his quill pen in the ink, or whatever
they used in those days, and setting out to draw a thorough
black-hearted villain. But to do it, he had to go all the way
with Iago, he had to go along with him and go down into
the depths with him, he had to feel what Iago felt. And
that's why when retribution comes, when Iago is for it,
Shakespeare saves his pride for him. He lets him keep the
only thing he's got left—his reticence. Shakespeare's been
down among the dead men himself. He knows that when
you've been in Hell, you don't talk about it . . ."

Gabriel wheeled round. His queer ugly face was con-
torted, his eyes shone with an odd kind of sincerity.

"You know, Norreys, I've never been able to believe
in God. God the father, who made the pretty beasts and
flowers, God who loves us and takes care of us, God who
created the world. No, I don't believe in that God. But
sometimes—I can't help it—I do believe in Christ . . . be-

cause Christ descended into Hell . . . His love went as deep as that. . . .

"He promised the repentant thief paradise. But what about the other one? The one who cursed and reviled him. Christ went with him down into Hell. Perhaps after that—"

Suddenly Gabriel shivered. He shook himself. His eyes became once more just rather beautiful eyes in an ugly face.

"I've been talking too much," he said. "Goodbye."

He departed abruptly.

I wondered whether he had been talking about Shakespeare or about himself. I thought, just a little, about himself. . . .

CHAPTER TWENTY

Gabriel had been confident about the result of the election. He had said that he did not see what could go wrong.

The unforeseen in this case was a girl called Poppy Narracott. She was the barmaid at the Smugglers Arms at Greatwithiel. She was a girl whom John Gabriel had never seen and did not know existed. Yet it was Poppy Narracott who set the events in motion which placed Gabriel's chances of election in real jeopardy.

For James Burt and Poppy Narracott were on very close terms. But James Burt, when he had taken too much drink, was rough—sadistically rough. The girl Poppy turned against him. She refused, categorically, to have anything more to do with him, and she stuck to her decision.

Which was why James Burt came home one night rolling drunk and in a raging temper and was further infuriated by the terrified demeanor of his wife Milly. He let himself go. All the fury and balked desire that he felt for Poppy he vented on his wretched wife. He behaved like a complete madman and Milly Burt, small blame to her, lost her head completely.

She thought Jim Burt would kill her.

Twisting herself out of his grasp, she rushed out of the

front door into the street. She had no idea of where she was going or to whom to go. To go to the police station would never have occurred to her. There were no near neighbors, only shops closely shuttered at night.

She had nothing but instinct to guide her fleeting footsteps. Instinct took her to the man she loved—the man who had been kind to her. There was no conscious thought in her head, no realization that scandal might result, she was terrified and she ran to John Gabriel. She was a desperate hunted animal looking for sanctuary.

She ran, disheveled and breathless, into the Kings Arms, and to the Kings Arms James Burt pursued her, roaring out threats of vengeance.

Gabriel, as it happened, was in the hall.

Personally, I don't see that John Gabriel could have behaved in any other way than he did. She was a woman he liked, he was sorry for her, and her husband was both drunk and dangerous. When James Burt came roaring in and swore at him and told him to give up his wife, accusing him point blank of being on terms of intimacy with her, Gabriel told him to go to hell, that he wasn't fit to have a wife, and that he, John Gabriel, was going to see that she was kept safe from him.

James Burt went for Gabriel like a charging bull and Gabriel knocked him down. After that he engaged a room for Mrs. Burt and told her to stay in it and lock her door. She couldn't possibly go back home now, he told her, and everything would come right in the morning.

By the next morning the news was all round St. Loo. Jim Burt had "found out" about his wife and Major Gabriel. And Gabriel and Mrs. Burt were staying together at the Kings Arms.

You can imagine, perhaps, the effect of this on the eve of the poll. Polling day was in two days' time.

"He's done for himself now," Carslake murmured distractedly. He walked up and down my sitting room. "We're finished—licked—Wilbraham's bound to get in. It's a disaster—a tragedy. I never liked the fellow. Hairy at the heel. I knew he'd end by letting us down."

Mrs. Carslake, in refined accents, lamented, "That's

what comes of having a candidate who isn't a gentleman."

My brother seldom took part in our political discussions. If he was present at all he smoked a pipe in silence. But on this occasion, he took his pipe out of his mouth and spoke.

"Trouble is," he said, "he *has* behaved like a gentleman."

It seemed to me then that it was an ironical thought that Gabriel's more blatant lapses from accepted gentlemanly standards had only increased his standing, but that his isolated piece of quixotic chivalry should be the circumstance to lay him low.

Presently Gabriel himself came in. He was dogged and unrepentant.

"No good making a song and dance about it, Carslake," he said. "Just tell me what the hell else I could do."

Carslake asked where Mrs. Burt was now.

Gabriel said she was still at the Kings Arms. He didn't see, he said, where else she was to go. And anyway, he added, it was too late. He whirled on Teresa whom he seemed to consider the realist of the assembly. "Isn't it?" he demanded.

Teresa said certainly it was too late.

"A night's a night," said Gabriel. "And it's nights people are interested in, not days."

"Really, Major Gabriel . . ." Carslake spluttered. He was shocked to the core.

"God, what a filthy mind you've got," said Gabriel. "I didn't spend the night with her, if that's what you're getting at. What I'm saying is that to the entire population of St. Loo it's the same thing. We were both at the Kings Arms."

That, he said, was all that people would mind about. That and the scene Burt had made and the things he went about saying about his wife and Gabriel.

"If she were to go away," said Carslake, "anywhere— just bundle her out of the place. Perhaps then——" He looked hopeful for a moment, then shook his head. "It would only look fishy," he said, "very fishy . . ."

"There's another thing to consider," said Gabriel. "What about her?"

Carslake stared at him uncomprehendingly.

"What do you mean?"

"You haven't thought of her side of it, have you?"

Carslake said loftily, "We really can't consider these minor points now. What we've got to try and find is some possibility of getting you out of this mess."

"Exactly," said Gabriel. "Mrs. Burt doesn't really count, does she? Who's Mrs. Burt? Nobody in particular. Only a wretched, decent girl who's been bullied and ill-treated and frightened half out of her wits and who's got nowhere to go and no money."

His voice rose.

"Well—I'll tell you this, Carslake. I don't like your attitude. And I'll tell you who Mrs. Burt is—she's a human being. To your blasted machine nobody and nothing matters but the election. That's what's always been rotten in politics. What did Mr. Baldwin say in the dark ages, 'If I had told the truth I should have lost the election.' Well, I'm not Mr. Baldwin—I'm nobody in particular. But what you're saying to me is, 'You've behaved like an ordinary human being so you'll lose the election!' All right then, to hell with the election! You can keep your damned creaking stinking election. I'm a human being first and a politician second. I've never said a word I shouldn't to that poor kid. I've never made love to her. I've been damned sorry for her, that's all. She came to me last night because she hadn't got anybody else to turn to. All right, she can stay with me. I'll look after her. And to hell with St. Loo and Westminster and the whole blasted business."

"Major Gabriel." It was Mrs. Carslake's fluting agonized voice. "You *can't* do a thing like that! Supposing Burt divorces her?"

"If he divorces her, I'll marry her."

Carslake said angrily, "You can't let us down like that, Gabriel. You can't flaunt this thing as an open scandal."

"Can't I, Carslake? You watch me." Gabriel's eyes were the angriest things I had ever seen. I had never liked him so well.

"You can't bully me. If a lot of tinpot electors vote for the principle that a man can knock his wife about and terrify her out of her senses and bring foul unfounded charges against her—well then, let 'em! If they want to vote for bare Christian decency they can vote for me."

"They won't though," said Teresa and she sighed.

Gabriel looked at her and his face softened.

"No," he said, "they won't."

Robert took his pipe out of his mouth again.

"More fools they," he said unexpectedly.

"Of course, Mr. Norreys, we know you're a Communist," said Mrs. Carslake acidly.

What she meant I have no idea.

Then into the midst of this seething bitterness stepped Isabella Charteris. She came through the window from the terrace. She was cool and grave and composed.

She paid no attention to what was going on. She had come to say something and she said it. She came right up to Gabriel as though he were alone in the room and spoke to him in a confidential voice.

"I think," she said, "it will be quite all right."

Gabriel stared at her. We all stared at her.

"About Mrs. Burt, I mean," said Isabella.

She displayed no embarrassment. She had instead the pleased air of a simple-minded person who thinks they have done the right thing.

"She's at the Castle," she went on.

"At the *Castle?*" said Carslake unbelievingly.

Isabella turned to him.

"Yes," she said. "As soon as we heard what had happened, I thought that would be much the best thing. I spoke to Aunt Adelaide and she agreed. We went straight in the car to the Kings Arms."

It had been, I discovered later, positively a Royal Progress. Isabella's quick brain had hit on the only possible counter move.

Old Lady St. Loo, as I have said, had tremendous ascendency in St. Loo. From her emanated, so to speak, correct Greenwich moral time. People might sneer and call her old-fashioned and reactionary, but they respected her, and where she approved no one was likely to disapprove.

She had driven up in the aged Daimler in state, Isabella with her. An indomitable figure, Lady St. Loo had marched into the Kings Arms and had asked for Mrs. Burt.

A red-eyed, tearful, shrinking Milly had in due course descended the stairs and had been received with a kind of Royal Accolade. Lady St. Loo had not minced her words or lowered her voice.

"My dear," she boomed, "I am more sorry than I can say to hear of what you have been through. Major Gabriel should have brought you to us last night—but he is so considerate that he did not like to disturb us. so late, I suppose."

"I—I—you are very kind."

"Get your things together, my dear. I will take you back with me now."

Milly Burt flushed and murmured that she hadn't—really—any things . . .

"Stupid of me," said Lady St. Loo. "We will stop at your house and get them."

"But—" Milly shrank . . .

"Get into the car. We will stop at your house and get them."

Milly bowed her head to superior authority. The three women got into the Daimler. It stopped a few yards further down Fore Street.

Lady St. Loo got out with Milly and accompanied her into the house. From the surgery James Burt, his eyes bloodshot, lurched out, prepared to break into a furious tirade.

He met old Lady St. Loo's eye and checked himself.

"Pack a few things, dear," said Lady St. Loo.

Milly fled upstairs quickly. Lady St. Loo addressed James Burt.

"You have behaved disgracefully to your wife," she said. "Quite disgracefully. The trouble with you is, Burt, that you drink too much. In any case you're not a nice man. I shall advise your wife to have nothing more to do with you. The things you have been saying about her are lies—and you know very well they are lies. Isn't that right?"

Her fierce eye hypnotized the twitching man.

"Oh well—I suppose—if you say so . . ."

"You know they are lies."

"All right—all right—I wasn't myself last night."

"Mind you let it be known they *were* lies. Otherwise I shall advise Major Gabriel to take proceedings. Ah, there you are, Mrs. Burt."

Milly Burt was descending the stairs with a small suitcase.

Lady St. Loo took her by the arm and turned to the door.

"Here—where's Milly going?" asked Milly's husband.

"She is coming with me to the Castle." She added militantly, "Have you anything to say to that?"

Burt shook his head vaguely. Lady St. Loo said sharply:

"My advice to you, James Burt, is to pull yourself together before it is too late. Stop drinking. Attend to your profession. You've got a good deal of skill. If you go on as you are going you will come to a very sticky end. Pull up, man. You can if you try. And curb that tongue of yours."

Then she and Milly got into the car. Milly sat beside Lady St. Loo. Isabella opposite them. They drove down the main street and along by the harbor and up by the market and so to the Castle. It was a Royal Progress and nearly everybody in St. Loo saw it.

That evening people were saying:

"It *must* be all right or Lady St. Loo wouldn't have her at the Castle."

Some people said that there was no smoke without fire and why should Milly Burt rush out of the house at night to Major Gabriel, and of course Lady St. Loo backed him up because of politics.

But the latter were in the minority. Character tells. Lady St. Loo had character. She had a reputation of absolute integrity. If Milly Burt was received at the Castle, if Lady St. Loo took her side, then Milly Burt was all right. Lady St. Loo wouldn't stand for anything else. Not old Lady St. Loo. Why, she was ever so particular!

The bare outline of these happenings was told to us by Isabella. She had come over from the Castle as soon as Milly was installed there.

As Carslake grasped the significance of what she was saying, his gloomy face brightened. He slapped his leg.

"My God," he said. "I believe it will do the trick. The old lady's smart. Yes, she's smart. Clever idea."

But the cleverness and the idea had been Isabella's. It amazed me how quick she had been to grasp the situation and to act.

"I'll get busy right away," said Carslake. "We must follow this up. Outline what our story's to be exactly. Come on, Janet. Major Gabriel—"

"I'll come in a minute," said Gabriel.

The Carslakes went out. Gabriel went closer to Isabella.

"You did this," he said. "Why?"

She stared at him—puzzled.

"But—because of the election."

"You mean you—you care very much that the Conservatives shall get in?"

She looked at him with surprise.

"No. I mean *you.*"

"Me?"

"Yes. You want to win the election very much, don't you?"

A queer bewildered look came over Gabriel's face. He turned away. He said—more to himself than to her or to any of us:

"Do I? I wonder. . . ."

CHAPTER TWENTY-ONE

As I have said before, this is not an accurate account of a political campaign. I was out of the main stream, in a backwater where I only caught echoes of what went on. I was aware of an increasing sense of urgency, which seemed to be striking everyone but myself.

There were two last frenzied days of electioneering. Gabriel came in twice during the time for a drink. When he relaxed, he looked fagged out, his voice was hoarse with addressing open air meetings but though tired his vitality was unimpaired. He said very little to me, probably because he was saving both his voice and his energy.

He tossed off his drink and murmured, "What a hell of a life this is! The damn fool things you have to say to people. Serves 'em right that they're governed the way they are."

Teresa spent most of her time driving cars. The morning of Polling Day came with a gale driving in from the Atlantic. The wind howled and rain beat against the house.

Isabella dropped in early after breakfast. She wore a black mackintosh, her hair was wet, her eyes bright. An immense blue rosette was pinned to the mackintosh.

"I'm driving people to the polls all day," she said. "So's Rupert. I've suggested to Mrs. Burt that she should come over and see you. Do you mind? You'll be all alone, won't you?"

I didn't mind, though I had actually been quite contented at the prospect of a peaceful day with my books. I had had almost too much company lately.

For Isabella to show herself concerned about my solitary state seemed singularly unlike Isabella. It was as though she had suddenly shown signs of adopting her Aunt Agnes's attitude towards me.

"Love seems to be having a softening effect upon you, Isabella," I said disapprovingly. "Or did Lady Tressilian think of it?"

Isabella smiled.

"Aunt Agnes wanted to come and sit with you herself," she said. "She thought it might be lonely for you and —what was it she said—that you might feel out of things."

She looked at me inquiringly. It was an idea, I saw, that would not have entered her own head.

"You don't agree?" I asked.

Isabella replied with her usual candor, "Well, you are out of things."

"Admirably true."

"I'm sorry if you mind about it, but I don't see that Aunt Agnes coming and breathing over you would make it any better. It would only mean that she would be out of things, too."

"And I'm sure she would like to be in things."

"I suggested Mrs. Burt coming because she's got to keep out of the way anyway. And I thought you might talk to her, perhaps."

"Talk to her?"

"Yes." A slight frown appeared on Isabella's white forehead. "You see, I'm no good at—at talking to people. Or letting them talk to me. She goes on and on."

"Mrs. Burt goes on and on?"

"Yes, and it seems so senseless—but I can't put things properly. I thought perhaps you could."

"What does she go on and on about?"

Isabella sat down on the arm of a chair. She spoke slowly, frowning a little, and giving a very good imitation of a traveler describing the more puzzling rites of some savage tribe.

"About what happened. About rushing to Major Gabriel. About its being all her fault. That if he loses the election she will be to blame. That if only she'd been more careful to begin with—that she ought to have seen what it might lead to. That if she'd been nicer to James Burt and understood him better, he might never have drunk so much. That she blames herself dreadfully and that she lies awake at night worrying about it and wishing she'd acted differently. That if she's injured Major Gabriel's career she'll never forgive herself as long as she lives. That nobody is to blame but her. That everything, always, has been her fault."

Isabella stopped. She looked at me. She was presenting me, as it were, on a platter, something that was to her quite incomprehensible.

A faint echo from the past came to me. Jennifer, knitting her adorable brows and shouldering manfully the blame for what other people had done.

I had thought it one of Jennifer's more lovable traits. Now, when Milly Burt was indulging in the same attitude, I saw that such a point of view might be distinctly irritating. Which, I reflected cynically, was the difference between thinking someone was a nice little woman, and being in love!

"Well," I said thoughtfully, "I suppose she might very well feel that way. Don't you?"

Isabella replied with one of her definite monosyllables.

"No," she said.

"But why not? Explain yourself."

"You know," said Isabella reproachfully, "that I can't say things." She paused, frowned and then began to speak —rather doubtfully. She said, "Things either have happened, or they haven't happened. I can see that you might worry beforehand—"

Even that, I could see, was not a really acceptable position to Isabella.

"But to go on worrying now—oh, it's as if you went for a walk in the fields and stepped in a cow pat. I mean, it wouldn't be any use spending the whole of the walk talking about it, wishing you hadn't stepped in the cow pat, that you'd gone another way, saying that it was all because you hadn't been looking where you were stepping, and that you always did do silly things like that. After all, the cow pat's there on your shoe—you can't get away from it—but you needn't have it in your *mind* as well! There's everything else—the fields and the sky and the hedges and the person you're walking with—they're all there too. The only time you've got to think about the cow pat again is when you actually get home when you have to deal with your shoe. Then you do have to think about it—"

Extravagance in self-blame was an interesting field on which to speculate. I could see that it was something in which Milly Burt might indulge rather freely. But I didn't really know why some people were more prone to it than others. Teresa had once implied that people like myself, who insisted on cheering people up, and putting things right, were not really being as helpful as they thought themselves. But that still didn't touch the question of why human beings enjoyed exaggerating their responsibility for events.

Isabella said hopefully, "I thought you could talk to her?"

"Supposing she likes—well, blaming herself," I said. "Why shouldn't she?"

"Because I think it makes it rather dreadful for *him*—for Major Gabriel. It must be very tiring having to go on and on assuring someone that it's quite all right."

It would undoubtedly, I thought to myself, be very tiring . . . It had been tiring, I remembered. . . . Jennifer had always been excessively tiring. But Jennifer had also had a lovely sweep of blue black hair, big sad gray eyes and the most adorable and ridiculous nose. . . .

Possibly John Gabriel enjoyed Milly's chestnut hair and soft brown eyes and didn't mind assuring her that it was quite all right.

"Has Mrs. Burt any plans?" I asked.

"Oh yes. Grandmother has found her a post in Sussex, as a companion housekeeper to someone she knows. It will be quite well paid and very little work. And there is a good train service to London, so that she can go up and meet her friends."

By friends, did Isabella, I wondered, mean Major John Gabriel? Milly was in love with Gabriel. I wondered if Gabriel was a little in love with her. I rather thought he might be.

"She could divorce Mr. Burt, I think," said Isabella. "Only divorce is expensive."

She got up, "I must go now. You will talk to her, won't you?" She paused by the door. "Rupert and I are being married a week today," she said softly. "Do you think you could come to the church? The scouts could push you there if it's a fine day."

"Would you like me to come?"

"Yes, I would—very much."

"Then I will."

"Thank you. We shall have a week together before he goes back to Burma. But I don't think the war will last very much longer, do you?"

"Are you happy, Isabella?" I asked gently.

She nodded.

"It seems almost frightening—when a thing you've

thought about for a long time really comes true . . . Rupert was there in my mind but getting so faint . . ."

She looked at me.   ..

"Even though it is all real—it doesn't *seem* real yet. I still feel I might—wake up. It's like a dream. . . ."

She added very softly, "To have everything . . . Rupert . . . St. Loo . . . all one's wishes come true . . ."

Then, with a start, she cried, "I oughtn't to have stayed so long. They gave me twenty minutes off for a cup of tea."

I gathered that I had been Isabella's cup of tea.

Milly Burt came over to see me in the afternoon. When she had struggled out of her mackintosh and pixie hood and galoshes, she smoothed her brown hair back and powdered her nose a little self-consciously and came to sit beside me. She was really, I thought, very pretty and also very nice. You couldn't dislike Milly Burt even if you wanted to, and I, for one, didn't want to.

"I hope you don't feel dreadfully neglected?" she said. "Have you had lunch and everything all right?"

I assured her that my creature comforts had been attended to.

"Later," I said, "we'll have a cup of tea."

"That will be very nice." She moved restlessly. "Oh, Captain Norreys, you do think he'll get in, don't you?"

"Too early to say."

"Oh, but I mean what do you think?"

"I'm sure he stands a very good chance," I said soothingly.

"It would have been a certainty but for me! How I could be so stupid—so *wicked*. Oh, Captain Norreys, I just think about it all the time. I blame myself *dreadfully*."

Here we go, I thought.

"I should stop thinking about it," I advised.

"But how can I?" Her large pathetic brown eyes opened wide.

"By the exercise of self-control and will power," I said.

Milly looked highly skeptical and slightly disapproving.

"I don't feel I *ought* to take it lightly. Not when it's been all my fault."

"My dear girl, your brooding over it won't help Gabriel to get into Parliament."

"No-o, of course not. . . . But I shall never forgive myself if I've injured his career."

We argued on familiar lines. I had been through a lot of this with Jennifer. There was the difference that I was now arguing in cold blood, unaffected by the personal equation of romantic susceptibility. It was a big difference. I liked Milly Burt—but I found her quite infuriating.

"For God's sake," I exclaimed, "don't make such a song and dance about it! For Gabriel's sake if nobody else's."

"But its for *his* sake I mind."

"Don't you think the poor fellow has enough on his back without your adding a load of tears and remorse?"

"But if he loses the election—"

"If he loses the election (which he hasn't lost yet) and if you've contributed to that result (which there is no means of knowing and which mayn't be so at all) won't it be disappointing enough for him to have lost the fight without having a remorseful woman piling her remorse on to make things worse?"

She looked bewildered and obstinate.

"But I want to make up for what I've done."

"Probably you can't. If you can, it will only be by managing to convince Gabriel that losing the election is a marvelous break for him, and that it has set him free for a much more interesting attack upon life."

Milly Burt looked scared.

"Oh," she said. "I don't think I could possibly do *that*."

I didn't think she could, either. A resourceful and unscrupulous woman could have done it. Teresa, if she had happened to care for John Gabriel, could have done it quite well.

Teresa's method with life is, I think, ceaseless attack.

Milly Burt's was, undoubtedly, ceaseless picturesque defeat. But then possibly John Gabriel liked picking up pieces and putting them together again. I had once liked that kind of thing myself.

"You're very fond of him, aren't you?" I asked.

Tears came into her brown eyes.

"Oh, I am . . . I am indeed. He's—I've never met anyone quite like him . . ."

I hadn't met anyone like John Gabriel myself, not that it affected me as it did Milly Burt.

"I'd do anything for him, Captain Norreys—I would indeed."

"If you care very much for him, that is something in itself. Just leave it at that."

Who had said "Love 'em and leave 'em alone"? Some psychologist writing advice to mothers? But there was a lot of wisdom in it applied to others beside children. But can we, really, leave anybody alone? Our enemies, perhaps, by an effort. But those we love?

I desisted from what has been termed unprofitable speculation and rang the bell and ordered tea.

Over tea I talked determinedly of films I remembered from last year. Milly liked going to the pictures. She brought me up-to-date with descriptions of the latest masterpieces. It was all quite pleasant and I enjoyed it, and I was quite sorry when Milly left me.

The far flung battle line returned at varying hours. They were weary and in differing moods of optimism and despair. Robert alone returned in normal and cheerful mood. He had found a fallen beech tree in a disused quarry and it had been exactly what his soul had been longing for. He had also had an unusually good lunch at a small pub. Subjects to paint and food are Robert's main topics of conversation. And not at all bad topics, either.

CHAPTER TWENTY-TWO

It was late the following evening when Teresa came abruptly into the room, pushed back her dark hair from her tired face and said, "Well, *he's in!*"

"What majority?" I asked.

"Two hundred and fourteen."

I gave a whistle.

"A near thing, then."

"Yes, Carslake thinks that if it hadn't been for the Milly Burt business, he'd have had at least a thousand."

"Carslake doesn't know what he's talking about more than anybody else."

"It's a terrific sweep to the Left all over the country. Labour's in everywhere. Ours will be one of the few Conservative gains."

"Gabriel was right," I said. "He prophesied that, you remember."

"I know. His judgment's uncanny."

"Well," I said, "little Milly Burt will go to bed happy tonight. She hasn't gummed up the works after all. What a relief that will be to her."

"Will it?"

"What a cat you are, Teresa," I said. "The little thing's devoted to Gabriel."

"I know she is." She added thoughtfully, "They suit each other, too. I think he might be reasonably happy with her—that is, if he wants to be happy. Some people don't."

"I've never noticed anything unduly ascetic about John Gabriel," I said. "I should say he thought of very little beyond doing himself well and grabbing as much as he can out of life. Anyway, he's going to marry money. He told me so. I expect he will too. He's clearly marked for success —the grosser forms of success. As for Milly, she seems obviously cast for the rôle of victim. Now, I suppose, you'll tell me she enjoys it, Teresa."

"No, of course not. But it takes a really strong character, Hugh, to say 'I've made a complete ass of myself,' and laugh about it, and go on to the next thing. The weak have to have something to take hold of. They have to see their mistakes, not simply as a failure to cope, but as a definite fault, a tragic sin."

She added abruptly, "I don't believe in evil. All the harm in the world is caused by the weak—usually meaning well—and managing to appear in a wonderfully romantic light. I'm afraid of them. They're dangerous. They are like derelict ships that drift in the darkness and wreck the sound seaworthy craft."

I did not see Gabriel till the following day. He looked deflated and almost devoid of vitality. I hardly recognized him for the man I knew.

"Election hangover?" I suggested.

He groaned.

"You've said it. What a nauseating thing success is. Where's the best sherry?"

I told him and he helped himself.

"I don't suppose Wilbraham feels particularly elated by failure," I remarked.

Gabriel gave a pale grin.

"No, poor devil. Besides, he takes himself and politics quite seriously, I believe. Not too seriously, but seriously enough. Pity he's so wet."

"I suppose you said all the proper things to each other about a fair fight and good sportsmanship and all that?"

Gabriel grinned again.

"Oh, we went through the right drill. Carslake saw to that. What an ass that man is! Knows his job by heart— word perfect—and absolutely no intelligence behind it."

I raised my glass of sherry.

"Well," I said, "here's success to your future career. You're started now."

"Yes," said Gabriel without enthusiasm, "I'm started."

"You don't seem very cheerful about it?"

"Oh, it's just what you called it—election hangover. Life's always dull when you've licked the other fellow. But there will be plenty more battles to fight. You watch out for the way I'm going to force myself into the public eye."

"Labour's got a pretty hefty majority."

"I know. It's splendid."

"Really, Gabriel. Strange words for our new Tory M.P."

"Tory M.P. be hanged! I've got my chance now. Who have we got to put the Tory Party on its feet again? Winston's a grand old fighter of wars, especially when you're up against it. But he's too old to tackle a peace. Peace is tricky. Eden's a nice mealy-mouthed English gentleman—"

He proceeded, working through various well-known names of the Conservative Party.

"Not a constructive idea among them. They'll bleat against Nationalisation, and fall with glee upon the Socialists' mistakes. (And boy, will they make mistakes! They're a fat-headed crowd. Old diehards of Trades Unionists—and irresponsible theorists from Oxford.) Our side will do all the old Parliamentary tricks—like pathetic old dogs at a Fair. Yap yap yap first, then stand on their hind legs and revolve in a slow waltz."

"And where does John Gabriel come in, in this attractive picture of the Opposition?"

"You can't have D Day until you've got it thoroughly worked out to the last detail. Then—let it rip. I shall get hold of the young fellows—the people with new ideas who are normally 'agin the Government.' Sell 'em an idea, and go all out *for* that idea."

"What idea?"

Gabriel threw me an exasperated glance.

"You always get things the wrong way round. It doesn't matter a tuppenny ha'penny damn *what* idea! I could think up half a dozen any time I like. There are only two things that ever stir people politically. One is put something in their pockets. The other is the sort of idea that sounds as though it would make everything come right and which is extremely easy to grasp, noble but woolly—and which gives you a nice inner glow. Man likes to feel a noble animal as well as being a well paid one. You don't want too practical an idea, you know—just something humane and that isn't directed toward anyone you'll have to meet personally. Have you noticed how subscriptions will pour in for earthquake victims in Turkey or Armenia or somewhere? But nobody really wanted to take an evacuated child into their house, did they? That's human nature."

"I shall follow your career with great interest," I assured him.

"In twenty years' time you'll find me growing fat and living soft and probably regarded as a public benefactor," Gabriel told me.

"And then?"

"What do you mean by 'And then'?"

"I just wondered if you might be bored."

"Oh, I shall always find some racket or other—just for the fun of it."

I was always fascinated by the complete assurance with which Gabriel sketched out his life. I had come to have faith in the fulfillment of his prognostications. He had a knack, I thought, of being right. He had foreseen that the country would vote Labour. He had been sure of his own victory. His life would follow the course he now predicted, not deviating by a hair's breadth.

I said rather tritely, "So all's for the best in the best of possible worlds."

He frowned quickly and irritably, and said:

"What a way you've got of putting your finger on a sore spot, Norreys."

"Why, what's wrong?"

"Nothing's wrong . . . nothing, really." He was silent a moment, then went on. "Ever gone about with a thorn in your finger? Know how maddening it can be—nothing really ba?—but always reminding you—pricking you—hampering you . . ."

"What's the thorn?" I asked. "Milly Burt?"

He stared at me in astonishment. I saw it wasn't Milly Burt.

"She's all right," he said. "No harm done there luckily. I like her. I hope I'll see something of her in London. None of this beastly local gossip in London."

Then, a flush coming over his face, he tugged a package out of his pocket.

"I wonder if you'd have a look at this. Is it all right, do you think? Wedding present. For Isabella Charteris. Suppose I have to give her something. When is it? Next Thursday? Or do you think it's a damn fool kind of present."

I unrolled the package with great interest. What I found gave me a complete surprise. It was the last thing I would have expected John Gabriel to produce as a wedding present.

It was a book of hours—exquisitely and delicately illuminated. It was a thing that should have been in a museum.

"Don't know exactly what it is," said Gabriel. "Some Catholic business. Couple of hundred years old. But I felt— I don't know—I thought it seemed to go with her. Of course, if you think it's just silly—"

I hastened to reassure him.

"It's beautiful," I said. "A thing anyone would be glad to possess. It's a museum piece."

"Don't suppose it's the sort of thing she'll care for particularly but it rather fits with her, if you know what I mean—" I nodded. I did know. "And after all, I've got to give her something. Not that I like the girl. I've no use for her at all. Stuck up haughty bit of goods. She's managed to snaffle his Lordship all right. I wish her joy of that stuffed shirt."

"He's a good deal more than a stuffed shirt."

"Yes—as a matter of fact he is. At any rate, I've got to remain on good terms with them. As the local M.P. I shall dine at the Castle and go to the annual garden party and all that. I suppose old Lady St. Loo will have to move over to the Dower House now—that moldy ruin near the church. I should say that anyone who lives there will soon die of rheumatism."

He took back the illuminated missal and wrapped it up again.

"You really think that it's all right? That it will do?"

"A magnificent and most unusual present," I assured him.

Teresa came in. Gabriel said he was just going.

"What's the matter with him?" she asked me, when he had gone.

"Reaction, I suppose."

Teresa said, "It's more than that."

"I can't help feeling," I said, "that it's a pity he won the election. Failure might have had a sobering effect on him. As it is, he'll be blatant in a couple of years' time. By and large, he's a nasty bit of goods. But I rather fancy that he'll get to the top of the tree all right."

I suppose it was the word tree that roused Robert to speech. He had come in with Teresa but in his own inconspicuous way, so that, as usual, we were quite startled when he spoke.

"Oh no, he won't," he said.

We looked at him inquiringly.

"He won't get to the top of the tree," said Robert. "Not a chance of it, I should say—"

He wandered disconsolately round the room and asked why someone always had to hide his palette knife.

CHAPTER TWENTY-THREE

The wedding of Lord St. Loo to Isabella Charteris was fixed for Thursday. It was very early, about one in the morning, I suppose, when I heard footsteps outside the window on the terrace.

I had not been able to sleep. It was one of my bad nights with a good deal of pain.

I thought to myself that fancy plays queer tricks, for I could have sworn that they were Isabella's footsteps on the terrace outside.

Then I heard her voice.

"Can I come in, Hugh?"

The French windows were ajar as they always were unless there was a gale blowing. Isabella came in and I switched on the lamp by my couch. I still had a feeling that I was dreaming.

Isabella looked very tall. She had on a long dark tweed coat and a dark red scarf over her hair. Her face was grave, calm and rather sad.

I could not imagine what she could be doing here at this time of the night—or rather morning. But I felt vaguely alarmed.

I no longer had the impression that I was dreaming. In point of fact I felt exactly the opposite. I felt as though everything that had happened since Rupert St. Loo had come home was a dream, and this was the wakening.

I remembered Isabella saying, "I still feel I might wake up."

And I suddenly realized that that was what had happened to her. The girl who was standing by me was no longer in her dream—she had woken up.

And I remembered another thing—Robert saying that there had been no bad fairies at Rupert St. Loo's christening. I had asked him afterwards what he meant and he had replied, "Well, if there's not one bad fairy—where's your story?" That, perhaps, was what made Rupert St. Loo not quite real, in spite of his good looks, his intelligence, his "rightness."

All these things passed through my mind confusedly in the second or two that elapsed before Isabella said:

"I came to say goodbye to you, Hugh."

I stared at her stupidly.

"Goodbye?"

"Yes. You see, I'm going away . . ."

"Going away? With Rupert, you mean?"

"No. With John Gabriel. . . ."

I was conscious then of the strange duality of the human mind. Half of my brain was thunderstruck, unbelieving. What Isabella was saying seemed quite incredible—a thing so fantastic that it simply couldn't happen.

But somewhere, another part of me was not surprised. It was like an inner voice saying mockingly, "But surely, you've known this all along . . ." I remembered how, without turning her head, Isabella had known John Gabriel's step on the terrace. I remembered the look on her face when she had come up from the lower garden on the night of the whist drive, and the way she had acted so swiftly in the crisis of Milly Burt. I remembered her saying, "Rupert must come soon . . ." with a strange urgency in her voice.

She had been afraid then, afraid of what was happening to her.

I understood, very imperfectly, the dark urge that was driving her to Gabriel. For some reason or other the man had a strange quality of attraction for women. Teresa had told me so long ago . . .

Did Isabella love him? I doubted it. And I could see no happiness for her with a man like Gabriel—a man who desired her but did not love her.

On his part it was sheer madness. It would mean abandoning his political career. It would be the ruin of all his ambitions. I couldn't see why he was taking this crazy step.

Did he love her? I didn't think so. I thought that in a way he hated her. She was part of the things (the Castle, old Lady St. Loo) that had humiliated him ever since he came here. Was that the obscure reason for this act of insanity? Was he avenging that humiliation? Was he willing to smash up his own life if he could smash up the thing that had humiliated him? Was this the "common little boy" taking his revenge?

I loved Isabella. I knew that now. I loved her so much that I had been happy in her happiness—and she *had* been happy with Rupert in her dream come true—of life at St. Loo. . . . She had only feared that it might not be real—

What, then, was real? John Gabriel? No, what she was doing was madness. She must be stopped—pleaded with, persuaded.

The words rushed to my lips . . . but they remained unspoken. To this day I don't know why. . . .

The only reason I can think of is that Isabella—was Isabella.

I said nothing.

She stooped and kissed me. It was not a child's kiss. Her mouth was a woman's mouth. Her lips were cool and fresh, they pressed mine with a sweetness and intensity I shall never forget. It was like being kissed by a flower.

She said goodbye and she went away, out of the window —out of my life, to where John Gabriel was waiting for her.

And I did not try to stop her. . . .

CHAPTER TWENTY-FOUR

With the departure of John Gabriel and Isabella from St. Loo the first part of my story ends. I realize how much it is their story and not mine, because once they had gone I can remember little or nothing that happened. It is all vague and confused.

I had never been interested in the political side of our life in St. Loo. For me, it was only a back cloth against which the protagonists in the drama moved. But the political repercussions must have been—indeed, I know they were—quite far-reaching.

If John Gabriel had had any political conscience he would not, of course, have done what he did do. He would have been appalled at the prospect of letting his side down. For it did let it down. The local feeling aroused was so tremendous that pressure would have been brought to bear on him to make him resign his newly won seat if he had not resigned it without being asked. The affair brought great discredit on the Conservative Party. A man with traditions and a more delicate sense of honor would have been acutely sensitive to that. I don't think John Gabriel cared in the slightest. What he had been out for was his own career—by his crazy conduct he had wrecked this career. That was how he looked at it. He had spoken truly enough when he had prophesied that only a woman would be able to spoil his life. He had not in the least foreseen who that woman would be.

He was not fitted by temperament or upbringing to understand the shock and horror felt by people like Lady Tressilian and Mrs. Bigham Charteris. Lady Tressilian had been brought up to believe that to stand for election to Parliament was a duty owed by a man to his country. That was how her father had envisaged it.

Gabriel could not even have begun to appreciate such an attitude. The way he looked at it was that the Conservative Party had picked a dud when they picked him. It was a gamble—and they had lost. If things had taken a normal course they would have done very well for themselves. But there was always the hundredth chance—and the hundredth chance had happened.

Curiously enough the person who took exactly the same point of view as Gabriel was the dowager Lady St. Loo.

She spoke of it once and once only, in the drawing

room at Polnorth House when she was alone with Teresa and myself.

"We cannot," she said, "avoid our share of blame. We knew what the man was like. We nominated a man who was an outsider, who had no real beliefs, no traditions, no true integrity. We knew perfectly well that the man was an adventurer, nothing else. Because he had qualities that appeal to the masses, a good war record, a specious appeal, we accepted him. We were prepared to let him use us, because *we* were prepared to use him. We excused ourselves by saying that we were going with the times. But if there is any reality, any meaning, in the Conservative tradition, it must live up to its tradition. We must be represented by men who, if not brilliant, are sincere, who have a stake in the country, who are prepared to take responsibility for those under them, who are not ashamed or uneasy at calling themselves the upper classes, because they accept not only the privileges but the duties of an upper class."

It was the voice of a dying *régime* speaking. I did not agree with it, but I respected it. New ideas; a new way of life was being born, the old was being swept away, but as an example of the best of the old, Lady St. Loo stood firm. She had her place and would hold that place until her death.

Of Isabella she did not speak. There the wound had gone deep into the heart. For Isabella, in the old lady's uncompromising view, had betrayed her own class. For John Gabriel the old martinet could find excuses—he was of the lesser breed without the law—but Isabella had betrayed the citadel from within.

Though Lady St. Loo said nothing of Isabella, Lady Tressilian did. She talked to me, I think, because she could talk to no one else—and also because she felt that owing to my invalid state I did not count. She had an incorrigibly motherly feeling towards my helplessness, and I think she felt almost justified in talking to me as though I were indeed her son.

Adelaide, she said, was unapproachable. Maude snapped her head off and immediately went out with the dogs. That vast sentimental heart of Lady Tressilian's had to unburden itself.

She would have felt disloyal discussing the family with Teresa. She did not feel disloyal in discussing it with me, possibly because she knew I loved Isabella. She loved Isabella, loved her dearly, and she could not stop thinking about her, and being puzzled and bewildered by what she had done.

"It was so unlike her—so very unlike her, Hugh. I do feel that man must have bewitched her. A very dangerous man, I always thought. . . . And she seemed so happy—so perfectly happy—she and Rupert seemed made for each other. I can't understand it. They were happy—they really were. Didn't you think so, too?"

I said, feeling my way, that yes, I thought they had been happy. I wanted to add, but I did not think that Lady Tressilian would understand, that sometimes happiness is not enough. . . .

"I can't help feeling that that horrible man must have *enticed* her away—that somehow or other he hypnotized her. But Addie says no. She says that Isabella would never do anything unless she fully meant to do it. I don't know, I'm sure."

Lady St. Loo was, I thought, right there.

Lady Tressilian asked, "Do you think they are married? Where do you think they are?"

I asked if they had had no word from her.

"No. Nothing. Nothing but the letter Isabella left. It was written to Addie. She said that she didn't expect Addie would ever forgive her and that probably Addie was right. And she said, 'It is no good saying I am sorry for all the pain I shall cause. If I were really sorry I wouldn't do it. I think Rupert may understand, but perhaps not. I shall always love you all, even if I never see you again.'"

Lady Tressilian looked at me, her eyes full of tears.

"That poor boy—that poor poor boy. Dear Rupert—and we had all got so fond of him."

"I suppose he took it very hard?"

I had not seen Rupert St. Loo since Isabella's flight.

He had left St. Loo on the following day. I don't know where he went or what he did. A week later, he had rejoined his unit in Burma.

Lady Tressilian shook her head tearfully.

"He was so kind, so gentle to us all. But he didn't want to talk about it. Nobody wants to talk about it." She sighed. "But I can't help wondering where they are and what they are doing. Will they get married? Where will they live?"

Lady Tressilian's mind was essentially feminine. It was direct, practical, occupied with the events of daily life. I could see that already, nebulously, she was building up a picture of Isabella's domestic life—marriage, a house, children. She had forgiven easily. She loved Isabella. What Isabella had done was shocking. It was disgraceful. It had let the family down. But it was also romantic. And Lady Tressilian was nothing if not romantic.

As I say my memories of the next two years at St. Loo are vague. There was a by-election in which Mr. Wilbraham was returned by a large majority. I don't even remember who was the Conservative candidate—some country gentleman of blameless life and no mass appeal, I fancy. Politics, without John Gabriel, no longer held my attention. My own health began to occupy most of my thoughts. I went to a hospital and started a series of operations which left me no worse, if little better. Teresa and Robert remained on in Polnorth House. The three old ladies of St. Loo Castle left the Castle and moved into a small Victorian house with an attractive garden. The Castle was let for a year to some people from the North of England. Eighteen months later, Rupert St. Loo came back to England and married an American girl with money. They had, Teresa wrote me, great plans for the complete restoration of the Castle as soon as building regulations permitted. Illogically I hated to think of St. Loo Castle restored.

Where Gabriel and Isabella actually were and what Gabriel was doing—nobody knew.

In 1947 Robert had a successful show in London of his Cornish pictures.

At that time, great advances were being made in surgery. On the Continent various foreign surgeons had been doing remarkable things in cases like mine. One of the few advantages that war brings in its train is a leap forward in the alleviation of human suffering. My own surgeon in London was enthusiastic about the work done by a Jewish doctor in Slovakia. Working in the Underground movements during the war, he had made daring experiments and had achieved really spectacular results. In a case like mine, it was possible, so my own man thought, that he could attempt something which no English surgeon would undertake.

That was why in the Autumn of 1947 I traveled out to Zagrade to consult Dr. Crassvitch.

There is no need to go into details of my own history. Suffice to say that Dr. Crassvitch, whom I found a sensitive and clever surgeon, pronounced his belief that by an operation my condition could be immensely improved. It would be possible, he hoped, that I should be able to move about freely on crutches—instead of lying prone, a helpless shattered wreck. It was arranged that I should go into his clinic forthwith.

My hopes and his were realized. At the end of six months I emerged able, as he had promised, to walk with the aid of crutches. I cannot hope to describe how exciting it made life for me. I remained on in Zagrade—since I had to have manipulative treatment several times a week. On a summer evening I swung myself slowly and painfully along the Zagrade main street and came to anchor in a small open air café where I ordered beer.

It was then, looking across the occupied tables, that I saw John Gabriel.

It was a shock. I had not thought of him for some time. I had no idea that he was in this part of the world. But what was a worse shock was the appearance of the man.

He had gone down in the world. His face had always been slightly coarse but it was coarsened now almost out of recognition. It was bloated and unhealthy, the eyes bloodshot. At this very moment I realized that he was slightly drunk.

He looked across, saw me, and rising, came unsteadily over to my table.

"Well," he said, "look who's here! Last man in the world I'd have expected to see."

It would have given me enormous pleasure to have driven my fist into John Gabriel's face—but apart from the fact that I was not in fighting condition, I wanted to learn news of Isabella. I invited him to sit down and have a drink.

"Thanks, Norreys, I will. How's St. Loo and the ginger-bread Castle and all the old tabby cats?"

I told him that it was some time since I had been in St. Loo, that the Castle was let and that the three old ladies had moved out.

He said hopefully that that must have been a nasty pill for the Dowager to swallow. I said I thought that she had been glad to go. I told him that Rupert St. Loo was engaged to be married.

"In fact," said Gabriel, "everything's turned out very nicely for everybody."

I managed not to reply. I saw the old grin curving his mouth upwards.

"Come on, Norreys," he said. "Don't sit there looking as though you've swallowed a poker. Ask about her. That's what you want to know, isn't it?"

The trouble with Gabriel was that he always carried the war into the enemy's camp. I acknowledged defeat.

"How is Isabella?" I said.

"She's all right. I haven't done the characteristic seducer's act and abandoned her in a garret."

It became still more difficult for me to refrain from hitting Gabriel. He had always had the power of being offensive. He was far more offensive now that he had begun to go downhill.

"She's here in Zagrade?" I asked.

"Yes, you'd better come and call. Nice for her to see an old friend and hear the St. Loo news."

Would it be nice for her? I wondered. Was there some taint, some far off echo of sadism in Gabriel's voice?

I said, my voice slightly embarrassed, "Are you—married?"

His grin was positively fiendish.

"No, Norreys, we're not married. You can go back and tell that to the old bitch at St. Loo."

(Curious the way Lady St. Loo still rankled.)

"I'm not likely to mention the subject to her," I said coldly.

"It's like that, is it? Isabella's disgraced the family." He tilted his chair backwards. "Lord, I'd like to have seen their faces that morning—the morning when they found we'd gone off together."

"My God, you're a swine, Gabriel," I said, my self-control slipping.

He was not at all annoyed.

"Depends how you look at it," he said. "Your outlook on life is so very narrow, Norreys."

"At any rate I've got a few decent instincts," I said sharply.

"You're so English. I must introduce you to the wide cosmopolitan set in which Isabella and I move."

"You don't look frightfully well, if I may say so," I said.

"That's because I drink too much," said Gabriel promptly. "I'm a bit high now. But cheer up," he went on, "Isabella doesn't drink. I can't think why not—but she doesn't. She's still got that schoolgirl complexion. You'll enjoy seeing her again."

"I would like to see her," I said slowly, but I wasn't sure as I said it, if it was true.

Would I like to see her? Wouldn't it, really, be sheer pain? Did she want to see me? Probably not. If I could know how she felt. . . .

"No illegitimate brats, you'll be glad to hear," said Gabriel cheerfully.

I looked at him. He said softly:

"You do hate me, don't you, Norreys?"

"I think I've good reason to."

"I don't see it that way. You got a lot of entertainment

out of me at St. Loo. Oh yes, you did. Interest in my doings probably kept you from committing suicide. I should certainly have committed suicide in your place. It's no good hating me just because you are crazy about Isabella. Oh yes, you are. You were then and you are now. That's why you're sitting here pretending to be amicable and really loathing my guts."

"Isabella and I were friends," I said. "A thing I don't suppose you're capable of understanding."

"I didn't mean you made passes at her, old boy. I know that isn't your line of country. Soul affinity, and spiritual uplift. Well, it will be nice for her to see an old friend."

"I wonder," I said slowly. "Do you really think that she would like to see me?"

His demeanor changed. He scowled furiously.

"Why the devil not? Why shouldn't she want to see you?"

"I'm asking you," I said.

He said, "I'd like her to see you."

That grated on me. I said, "In this case, we'll go by what *she* prefers."

He suddenly beamed into a smile again.

"Of course she'll want to see you, old boy. I was just ragging you. I'll give you the address. Look her up any time you like. She's usually in."

"What are you doing nowadays?" I asked.

He winked, closing one eye and tilting his head sideways.

"Undercover work, old boy. Very hush hush. Poorly paid, though. £1,000 a year I'd be getting now as an M.P. (I told you if Labour got in it would go up.) I often remind Isabella how much I've given up for her sake."

How I loathed that coarse jeering devil. I wanted to— well, I wanted to do many things that were physically impossible to me. Instead, I contained myself and accepted the bit of dirty paper with the address scrawled on it that he shoved across to me.

It was a long time before I could get to sleep that night. I was beset by fears for Isabella. I wondered if it was possible to get her to leave Gabriel. Obviously the whole thing had turned out badly.

How badly I only realized on the following day. I found the address that Gabriel had given me. It was a disreputable-looking house in a mean back street. That quarter of the town was a bad one. The furtive men and the brazen painted women I passed told me that. I found the house and asked, in German, of a vast blowsy woman who was standing in the doorway, for the English lady.

She understood German fortunately, and directed me to the top floor. I climbed with difficulty, my crutches slipping. The house was filthy. It smelt. My heart dropped down into my boots. My beautiful proud Isabella. To have come down to this. But at the same time my own resolve strengthened.

I would get her out of all this. Take her back to England. . . .

I arrived, panting, on the top floor, and knocked on the door.

A voice called out something in Czech from inside. I knew that voice—it was Isabella's. I opened the door and went in.

I don't think I can ever explain the extraordinary effect that room had on me.

To begin with, it was definitely squalid. Broken down furniture, tawdry hangings, an unpleasant-looking and somehow lewd brass bedstead. The place was at once clean and dirty; that is, the walls were streaked with dirt, the ceiling black, and there was the faint unpleasant odor of bugs. There was no surface dirt. The bed was made, the ashtrays empty, there was no litter and no dust.

But it was nevertheless a sordid room. In the middle of it, sitting with her feet tucked up under her, and embroidering a piece of silk, was Isabella.

She looked exactly as she had looked when she left St. Loo. Her dress, actually, was shabby. But it had cut and style, and though old, she wore it with ease and distinction. Her hair was still in its long shimmering page-boy bob. Her face was beautiful, calm, and grave. She and the room had, I felt, nothing to do with each other. She was here, in

the midst of it, exactly as she might have been in the midst
of a desert, or on the deck of a ship. It was not her home.
It was a place where she happened, just at the moment, to
be.

She stared for a second, then, jumping up, came towards me with a glad surprised face, her hands out-
stretched. I saw then, that Gabriel had not told her of my
being in Zagrade. I wondered why.

Her hands came affectionately into mine. She raised
her face and kissed me.

"Hugh, how lovely."

She did not ask how I happened to be in Zagrade. She
did not comment on the fact that I could now walk whereas
when she had last seen me I was prone on a couch. All that
concerned her was that her friend had come, and that she
was glad to see him. She was, in fact, my Isabella.

She found a chair for me and drew it up to her own.

"Well, Isabella," I said, "what are you doing with yourself?"

Her reply was typical. She immediately showed me her
embroidery.

"I began it three weeks ago. Do you like it?"

Her voice was anxious.

I took the piece of work into my hand. It was a square
of old silk—a delicate dove gray in color, slightly faded,
very soft to handle. On it Isabella was embroidering a design of dark red roses, wallflowers and pale mauve stocks.
It was beautiful work, very fine, exquisitely executed.

"It's lovely, Isabella," I said, "quite lovely."

I felt as always the strange fairy story quality that always
surrounded Isabella. Here was the captive maiden doing
fine embroidery in the ogre's tower.

"It's beautiful," I said, handing it back to her. "But
this place is awful."

She looked round with a casual, almost surprised, glance.

"Yes," she said. "I suppose it is."

Just that, no more. It baffled me—as Isabella had always baffled me. I saw vaguely that it mattered very little
to Isabella what her surroundings were. She was not thinking of them. They mattered to her no more than the up-

holstery or decorations in a railway train matters to someone who is engaged upon an important journey. This room was the place she happened to be living in at the moment. Her attention drawn to it, she agreed that it was not a nice place, but the fact did not really interest her.

Her embroidery interested her far more.

I said, "I saw John Gabriel last night."

"Did you? Where? He didn't tell me."

I said, "That's how I got your address. He invited me to come and look you up."

"I'm so glad you did. Oh, I *am* glad!"

How warming it was—her eager pleasure in my presence.

"Isabella—dear Isabella," I said. "Are you all right? Are you happy?"

She stared at me, as though doubtful of my meaning.

"All this," I said. "It's so different from what you've been used to. Wouldn't you like to leave it all—to come back with me. To London if not to St. Loo."

She shook her head.

"John's doing something here. I don't know what exactly—"

"What I'm trying to ask you is if you're happy with him? I don't think you can be . . . If you once made a dreadful mistake, Isabella, don't be too proud to own it now. Leave him."

She looked down at her work—strangely, a little smile hovered on her lips.

"Oh no, I couldn't do that."

"Do you love him so much, Isabella? Are you—are you really happy with him? I ask because I care for you so much."

She said gravely, "You mean happy—happy in the way I was happy at St. Loo?"

"Yes."

"No, of course I'm not . . ."

"Then chuck it all up, come back with me and start afresh."

Again she gave that funny little smile.

"Oh no, I couldn't do that."

"After all," I said, rather embarrassed, "you're not married to him."

"No, I'm not married. . . ."

"Don't you think—" I felt awkward—embarrassed—all the things that so palpably Isabella was not. Still, I had to find out exactly how matters stood between these two strange people. "Why aren't you married?" I said brazenly.

She was not offended. I had, instead, the impression that it was the first time the question had presented itself to her. Why was it that she and John Gabriel were not married? She sat quite still, thoughtful, asking herself why?

Then she said, doubtfully, in a rather puzzled way:

"I don't think John—wants to marry me."

I managed not to explode into anger.

"Surely," I said, "there is no reason why you should *not* marry?"

"No," her tone was doubtful.

"He owes it to you. It is the least he can do."

She shook her head slowly.

"No," she said. "It was not like that at all."

"What was not like that?"

She brought the words out slowly, following up events in her mind.

"When I came away from St. Loo . . . it was not to marry John instead of marrying Rupert. He wanted me to come away with him, and I came. He didn't speak of marriage. I don't think he thought of it. All this—" she moved her hands slightly—by "this" I took it she meant not so much the actual rooms, the squalid surroundings, as the transitory character of their life together—"this isn't marriage. Marriage is something quite different."

"You and Rupert—" I began.

She interrupted me, relieved apparently that I had grasped her point.

"Yes," she said, "that would have been marriage."

Then what, I wondered, did she consider her life with John Gabriel to be? I didn't like to ask outright.

"Tell me, Isabella," I said. "What do you actually understand by marriage—what does marriage mean to you —apart from its pure legal significance?"

She was very thoughtful about that.

"I think it would mean becoming part of someone's life . . . fitting in . . . taking your place . . . and its being your rightful place—where you belong."

Marriage to Isabella had, I saw, a structural significance. "You mean," I said, "that you can't share Gabriel's life?"

"No. I don't know how. I wish I could. You see—" she stretched out her long narrow hands in front of her— "I don't know anything about him."

I stared at her, fascinated. I thought that she was instinctively right. She did not know the first thing about John Gabriel. She never would know the first thing about him, however long she stayed with him. But I could see, also, that that might not affect her emotional feeling for him.

And he, I thought suddenly, was in the same boat. He was like a man who had bought (or rather had looted) an expensive and delicate piece of craftsmanship and who had no conception of the scientific principles underlying its elaborate mechanism.

"So long," I said slowly, "as you are not unhappy."

She looked back at me with blind unseeing eyes. Either she deliberately concealed the answer to my question, or she did not know the answer herself. I think the latter. She was living through a deep and poignant experience, and she could not define it for my benefit in exact terms.

I said gently, "Shall I give them your love at St. Loo?"

She sat very still. Tears came up in her eyes and spilled. They were tears not of sorrow but of remembrance.

"If you could put the clock back, Isabella," I said. "If you were free to choose—would you make the same choice again?"

It was cruel of me, perhaps, but I had to know, to be sure.

But she looked at me without comprehension.

"Does one ever really have any choice? About anything?"

Well, that is a matter of opinion. Life is easier, perhaps, for uncompromising realists like Isabella Charteris who cannot perceive any alternative way. Yet, as I now believe, there was to come a moment when Isabella had a definite choice and took one way in preference to the other with full knowledge that it was a choice. But that was not yet.

Then as I stood looking at Isabella I heard footsteps stumbling up the stairs. John Gabriel flung the door open with a flourish and lurched into the room. He was not a particularly pretty sight.

"Hullo," he said, "found your way here all right?"

"Yes," I said shortly.

For the life of me I couldn't say any more. I went toward the door.

"Sorry," I mumbled, "I've got to be going. . . ."

He stood aside a little to let me pass.

"Well," he said, and there was something in his expression that I didn't understand, "don't ever say I didn't give you your chance . . ."

I didn't know quite what he meant.

He went on, "Dine with us at the Café Gris tomorrow night. I'm throwing a party. Isabella would like you to come, wouldn't you, Isabella?"

I looked back. She was smiling at me gravely.

"Yes, do come," she said.

Her face was calm and unperturbed. She was smoothing and sorting her silks.

I caught a fleeting glimpse of something in Gabriel's face that I didn't understand. It might have been desperation.

I went down that horrid staircase quickly—as quickly as a cripple could go. I wanted to get out into the sunlight —away from the strange conjunction of Gabriel and Isabella. Gabriel had changed—for the worse. Isabella had not changed at all.

In my puzzled mind I felt that there must be some significance in that if only I could find it.

CHAPTER TWENTY-FIVE

There are some horrible memories you can never manage to forget. One of those was that nightmare evening in the Café Gris. I am convinced that that party was arranged entirely to satisfy Gabriel's malice towards me. It was, in my view, an infamous party. John Gabriel's friends and associates in Zagrade were introduced to me there—and in the midst of them sat Isabella. They were men and women she should never have been allowed to meet. There were drunkards and perverts, coarse-painted trollops, diseased dope addicts. Everything that was mean, base, and depraved.

And they were not redeemed, as might so easily have been the case, by artistic talent. Here were no writers, musicians, poets or painters; not even witty talkers. They were the dregs of the cosmopolitan world. They were Gabriel's choice. It was as though he had deliberately wished to show how low he could go.

I was wild with resentment for Isabella's sake. How dared he bring her into such a company?

And then I looked at her and resentment dropped from me. She showed no avoidance, no disgust, still less did she display any anxiety to gloss over a difficult situation. She sat there smiling quietly, the same remote Acropolis Maiden smile. She was gravely polite and quite untouched by her company. They did not, I saw, affect her—any more than the squalid lodgings in which she lived affected her. I remembered from long ago her answer to my question as to whether she was interested in politics. She had said then, looking a little vague, "It is one of the things we do." Tonight, I divined, came into the same category. If I had asked her what she felt about this party she would have said in the same tone, "It's the kind of party we have." She accepted it without resentment, and without any particular interest, as one of the things John Gabriel chose to do.

I looked across the table at her and she smiled back at

me. My agony and distress on her behalf were simply not needed. A flower can bloom as well on a dung heap as anywhere else. Perhaps better—for you notice that it is a flower. . . .

We left the Café in a body. Nearly everybody was drunk.

As we stepped into the street to cross it, a large car came noiselessly out of the darkness. It nearly hit Isabella, but she saw her danger in time and made a sudden leap for the pavement—I saw the whiteness of her face and the sharp terror in her eyes as the car went hooting down the street.

Here, then, she was still vulnerable. Life, in all its vicissitudes, was powerless to affect her. She could stand up to life—but not to death—or the threat of death. Even now, with the danger over, she was white and shaken.

Gabriel cried out:

"My God, that was a near shave. Are you all right, Isabella?"

She said, "Oh, yes! I'm all right."

But the fear was still in her voice. She looked at me and said, "You see, I'm still a coward."

There isn't very much more to tell. That evening at the Café Gris was the last time I was to see Isabella.

Tragedy came, as it usually comes, unheralded, without forewarning.

I was just wondering whether to go and see Isabella again, whether to write, whether to leave Zagrade without seeing her when Gabriel was shown in to see me.

I can't say that I noticed anything unusual in his appearance. A certain nervous excitement, perhaps, a tightness. I don't know. . . .

He said quite calmly, "Isabella's dead."

I stared at him. I didn't take it in at first. I simply didn't feel that it could be true.

He saw my disbelief.

"Oh yes," he said. "It's true. She was shot."

I found my tongue, as a cold sense of catastrophe—of utter loss—spread through me.

"Shot?" I said. *"Shot?* How could she be shot? How did it happen?"

He told me. They had been sitting together in the café where I had first met him.

He asked me, "Have you ever seen pictures of Stolanov? Do you see any likeness to me in him?"

Stolanov was at that time virtual dictator of Slovakia. I looked at Gabriel carefully and I realized that there was quite a strong facial resemblance. When Gabriel's hair fell forward untidily over his face, as it frequently did, that slight resemblance was heightened.

"What happened?" I asked.

"A damn fool of a student. He thought he recognized me as Stolanov. He had a revolver with him. He ran shooting across the café, yelling out 'Stolanov—Stolanov—I've got you at last.' There wasn't any time to do anything at all. He fired. He didn't hit me. He hit Isabella . . ."

He paused. Then added, "She was killed instantaneously. The bullet went through her heart."

"My God," I said, "and you couldn't do anything?"

It seemed to me incredible that Gabriel hadn't been able to do anything.

He flushed.

"No," he said. "I couldn't do anything . . . I was behind the table against the wall. There wasn't *time* to do anything . . ."

I was silent. I was still stunned—numb.

Gabriel sat watching me. He still showed no sign of emotion.

"So that's what you've brought her to," I said at last.

He shrugged his shoulders.

"Yes—if you like to put it that way."

"It's your doing that she was here—in that foul house, in this foul town. But for you she might have been—"

I stopped. He finished the sentence for me.

"She might have been Lady St. Loo, living in a castle by the sea—living in a gingerbread castle with a gingerbread husband and a gingerbread child on her knee, perhaps."

The sneer in his voice maddened me.

"My God, Gabriel," I said. "I don't think I shall ever forgive you!"

"I can't say it interests me very much, Norreys, if you forgive me or not."

"What are you doing here, anyway?" I asked angrily. "Why come to me? What do you want?"

He said quietly, "I want you to take her back to St. Loo . . . You can manage it, I expect. She ought to be buried there, not here where she doesn't belong."

"No," I said. "She doesn't belong here." I looked at him. In the midst of the pain I was beginning to feel I was aware of a rising curiosity.

"Why did you ever bring her away? What was the idea behind it all? Did you want her so much? Enough to chuck up your career? All the things you set so much store by?"

Again he shrugged his shoulders.

I cried angrily, "I don't understand!"

"Understand? Of course you don't understand." His voice startled me. It was hoarse and rasping. "You'll never understand anything. What do you know about suffering?"

"A good deal," I said, stung.

"No, you don't. You don't know what suffering, real suffering is. Don't you understand that I've never known —once—what she's been thinking . . . ? I've never been able to talk to her. I tell you, Norreys, I've done everything to break her spirit—everything. I've taken her through the mud—through the dregs—and I don't think she even knows what I've been doing! 'She can't soil and she can't scare.' That's what Isabella is like. It's frightening, I tell you, frightening. Rows, tears, defiance—that's what I'd always imagined. And myself winning! But I didn't win. You can't win when you're fighting someone who doesn't know there is a fight. And I couldn't talk to her—I could never talk to her. I've drunk myself paralytic, I've tried drugs, I've gone with other women. . . . It hasn't touched her. She's sat there with her feet tucked up, embroidering her silk flowers, and sometimes singing to herself. . . . She might be still in her castle by the sea—she's still in her blasted fairy story—she brought it with her—"

He had slid insensibly into the present tense. But he stopped suddenly. He dropped into a chair.

"You don't understand," he said. "How can you? Well, I'm licked. I've had her body. I've never had anything else. Now her body's escaped me. . . ." He got up. "Take her back to St. Loo."

"I will," I said. "And God forgive you, Gabriel, for what you've done to her!"

He swerved round on me.

"For what I've done to her? What about what she's done to me? Hasn't it ever penetrated your smug mind, Norreys, that from the first moment I saw that girl, I suffered tortures? I can't explain to you what the mere sight of her did to me—I don't understand it now. It was like chillis and cayenne pepper rubbed into a raw wound. All the things I'd wanted and minded about all my life seemed to crystallize in her. I knew I was coarse, filthy, sensual—but I didn't mind about it till I saw her.

"She hurt me, Norreys. Don't you understand? She hurt me as nothing had ever hurt me before. I had to destroy her—to pull her down to my level. Don't you see—no, you don't! You don't understand anything. You're incapable of it. You curl yourself up in the window-seat as though life were a book you were reading! I was in Hell, I tell you, in *Hell*.

"Once, just once, I thought I'd got a break—a loophole of escape. When that nice silly little woman came bolting into the St. Loo Arms and jammed up the works. It meant that the election was dished, and I was dished. I'd have Milly Burt on my hands. That brute of a husband of hers would have divorced her, and I'd have done the decent thing and married her. Then I'd have been safe. Safe from this awful torturing obsession . . .

"And then she, Isabella herself, took a hand. She didn't know what she was doing to me. I'd got to go on! There was no escape. I hoped, all along, that I'd just pull through. I even bought her a wedding present.

"Well, it was no use. I couldn't stick it. I had to have her . . ."

"And now," I said, "she's dead. . . ."

This time he let me have the last word.

He repeated, very softly, "And now—she's dead . . ."

He turned on his heel and went out of the room.

CHAPTER TWENTY-SIX

That was the last time I saw John Gabriel. We parted in anger in Zagrade and did not meet again.

With some difficulty I made the arrangements which permitted Isabella's body to be brought home to England.

She was buried in the small churchyard by the sea at St. Loo where the other members of her family are buried. After the funeral, I went back with the three old ladies to the little Victorian house and was thanked by them for bringing Isabella home. . . .

They had aged terribly in the last two years. Lady St. Loo was more like an eagle than ever, her flesh stretched tightly over her bones. She looked so frail that I thought she might die any moment. Actually, though, she lived for many years after that. Lady Tressilian was stouter and very asthmatic. She told me in a whisper that they all liked Rupert's wife very much.

"Such a practical girl and so bright. I'm sure they'll be happy. Of course it isn't what we once dreamed of . . ."

The tears came into her eyes. She murmured, "Oh why —why did this have to happen?"

It was an echo of what had never ceased to reiterate in my own brain.

"That wicked—wicked man . . ." she went on.

We were united, three old ladies and myself in our sorrow for a dead girl and our hatred of John Gabriel.

Mrs. Bigham Charteris was more leathery than ever. She said as I finally bid them goodbye, "Do you remember little Mrs. Burt?"

"Yes, of course. What's happened to her?"

Mrs. Bigham Charteris shook her head.

"I'm sadly afraid she's going to make a fool of herself. You know what happened to Burt?"

"No, I don't."

"Upset into a ditch one night when he'd had one over the eight. Struck his head on a stone. Killed him."

"So she's a widow?"

"Yes. And I hear from my friends in Sussex that she's taken up with one of the farmers near there. Going to marry him. Man has a bad reputation. Drinks. Bit of a bully too."

So Milly Burt, I thought, was repeating her pattern . . .

Did anyone ever profit by having a second chance . . . ?

I wondered more than ever when I was on my way to London the following day. I had boarded the train at Penzance and taken a ticket for first lunch. As I sat there waiting for the soup to be served, I thought about Jennifer.

I had had news of her from time to time from Caro Strangeways. Jennifer, Caro had told me, was very unhappy. She had complicated her life in an incredible fashion, but she was being very plucky over it. One couldn't, Caro said, help admiring her.

I smiled a little to myself, thinking of Jennifer. Jennifer was rather a darling. But I felt no urge to see her—no real interest.

One doesn't care for hearing the same record too often. . . .

So I came at last to Teresa's house in London and Teresa let me talk . . .

She heard my bitter diatribes against John Gabriel. I described the happenings in Zagrade to her and ended with the account of Isabella's grave in St. Loo.

Then I was silent for a moment, hearing the noise of the Atlantic breakers against the rocks and seeing the outline of St. Loo Castle against the sky. . . .

"I suppose I ought to feel that I've left her there in peace—but I don't, Teresa. I'm full of rebellion. She died before her time. She said to me once that she hoped she would live to be a very old woman. She could have lived to be old. She was very strong. I think that's what I find so unendurable—that her life was cut short . . ."

Teresa stirred a little against the background of a large painted screen. She said:

"You're going by Time. But Time doesn't mean anything at all. Five minutes and a thousand years are equally significant." She quoted softly, "The moment of the Rose and the moment of the Yew Tree are of equal duration . . ."

(A dark red rose embroidered on faded gray silk. . . .)

Teresa went on, "You will insist on making your own design for life, Hugh, and trying to fit other people into it. But they've got their own design. Everyone has got their own design—that's what makes life so confusing. Because the designs are interlaced—superimposed.

"Just a few people are born clear-eyed enough to know their own design. I think Isabella was one of them. . . . She was difficult to understand—for *us* to understand—not because she was complex but because she was simple—almost terrifyingly simple. She recognized nothing but essentials.

"You persist in seeing Isabella's life as a thing cut short, twisted out of shape, broken off. . . . But I have a strong suspicion that it was a thing complete in itself . . ."

"The moment of the rose?"

"If you like to call it that." She added softly, "You're very lucky, Hugh."

"Lucky?" I stared at her.

"Yes, because you loved her."

"I suppose I did love her. And yet I never was able to do anything for her . . . I didn't even try to stop her going away with Gabriel . . ."

"No," said Teresa, "because you really loved her. You loved her enough to leave her alone."

Almost unwillingly I accepted Teresa's definition of love. Pity has always, perhaps, been my undoing. It has been my cherished indulgence. By pity, the facile easy going of pity, I have lived and warmed my heart.

But Isabella, at least, I had kept free of pity. I had never tried to serve her, to make her path easy for her, to carry her burdens. In her short life she was completely and perfectly herself. Pity is an emotion she neither needed, nor would have understood. As Teresa said, I had loved her enough to leave her alone . . .

"Dear Hugh," said Teresa gently, "of course you loved her. And you've been very happy loving her."

"Yes," I said, a little surprised. "Yes, I've been very happy."

Then anger swept over me.

"But," I said, "I still hope that John Gabriel will suffer the tortures of the damned in this world and the next!"

"I don't know about the next," said Teresa, "but in this world I should say that you had got your wish. John Gabriel is the most unhappy man I have ever known . . ."

"I suppose you're sorry for him, but I can tell you—"

Teresa interrupted. She said she wasn't exactly sorry for him. She said it went deeper than that.

"I don't know what you mean. If you'd seen him in Zagrade—he did nothing but talk about himself—he wasn't even broken up by Isabella's death."

"You don't know. I don't suppose you even looked at him properly. You never do look at people."

It struck me when she said that, that I had never really looked properly at Teresa. I have not even described her in this story.

I looked at her and it seemed to me that I was, perhaps, seeing her for the first time . . . seeing the high cheekbones and the upward sweep of black hair that seemed to need a mantilla and a big Spanish comb. Seeing that her head was set on her neck very proudly like her Castilian great grandmother's.

Looking at her, it seemed to me just for a moment that I saw exactly what Teresa must have been like as a young girl. Eager, passionate, stepping adventurously forward into life.

I did not know in the least what she had found there . . .

"Why are you staring at me, Hugh?"

I said slowly, "I was thinking that I had never looked at you properly."

"No, I don't think you have." She smiled faintly. "Well, what do you see?"

There was irony in her smile and laughter in her voice and something in her eyes that I could not fathom.

"You have been very good to me always, Teresa," I said

slowly. "But I don't really know anything about you . . ."

"No, Hugh. You know nothing at all."

She got up brusquely and pulled the curtain that was letting in too much sun.

"As to John Gabriel—" I began.

Teresa said in her deep voice, "Leave him to God, Hugh."

"That's an odd thing to say, Teresa."

"No, I think it's the right thing to say, I've always thought so."

She added, "One day—perhaps you'll know what I mean."

EPILOGUE

Well, that is the story.

The story of the man I first knew at St. Loo in Cornwall and whom I had last seen in a hotel room at Zagrade.

The man who was now dying in a back bedroom in Paris.

"Listen, Norreys," his voice was weak but clear. "You've got to know what really happened in Zagrade. I didn't tell you at the time. I think I hadn't really taken in what it meant . . ."

He paused, gathering breath.

"You know that she—Isabella—was afraid of dying? More afraid of it than anything else in the world?"

I nodded. Yes, I knew. I remembered the blind panic in her eyes when she had looked down at a dead bird on the terrace at St. Loo, and I remembered how she had leaped to avoid the car in Zagrade and the whiteness of her face.

"Then listen. *Listen,* Norreys: the student came for me with the revolver. He was only a few feet away. He couldn't miss. And I was pinned behind the table. I couldn't move.

"Isabella saw what was going to happen. *She flung herself in front of me as he pressed the trigger . . .*"

Gabriel's voice rose.

"Do you understand, Norreys? She knew what she was doing. She knew that it meant death—for her. She chose death—to save me."

Warmth came into his voice.

"I hadn't understood—not until then. I didn't realize even then, what it meant, until I came to think about it. I'd never understood, you see, that she *loved* me. . . . I thought—I was convinced—that I held her by her senses. . . .

"But Isabella loved me—she loved me so much that she gave her life for me—in spite of her fear of death. . . ."

My mind moved backward. I was in the café in Zagrade. I saw the fanatical hysterical young student, saw Isabella's sharp alarm, her realization, her momentary panic fear—and then her swift choice. I saw her fling herself forward shielding John Gabriel with her body. . . .

"So that was the end . . ." I said.

But Gabriel pulled himself up on his pillows. His eyes, those eyes that had always been beautiful, opened very wide. His voice rang out loud and clear—a triumphant voice.

"Oh no," he said, "that's where you are wrong! It wasn't the end. *It was the beginning. . . .*"

AGATHA CHRISTIE

"One of the most imaginative and fertile plot creators of all time!"—Ellery Queen

Miss Marple

____THE MURDER AT THE VICARAGE	0-425-09453-7/$3.50
____THE TUESDAY CLUB MURDERS	0-425-08903-7/$3.50
____DOUBLE SIN AND OTHER STORIES	0-425-06781-5/$3.50
____THE MOVING FINGER	0-425-10569-5/$3.50
____THE REGATTA MYSTERY AND OTHER STORIES	0-425-10041-3/$3.50
____THREE BLIND MICE AND OTHER STORIES	0-425-06806-4/$3.50

NGAIO MARSH

BESTSELLING PAPERBACKS BY A "GRAND MASTER" OF THE MYSTERY WRITERS OF AMERICA.